The
India
I dream of...

Books by the same author

When life tricked me..

The
India
I dream of...

Vikrant Khanna

Srishti
PUBLISHERS & DISTRIBUTORS

Srishti Publishers & Distributors
N-16, C. R. Park
New Delhi 110 019
srishtipublishers@gmail.com

First published by
Srishti Publishers & Distributors in 2012

Typeset by EGP at Srishti

Dedicated to all us Indians
who always crib and complain *

*and to others who don't!!!

PROLOGUE

I had never believed in the power of facebook. Hell I never even had an account until few months ago when Dev and Nikita – my best friends from school - coaxed me into having one. I had always thought it was meant for introverts who lived in an apparent world restricted within their own shell.

I mean how else could someone explain facebook chatting with people whom you never even meet or talk in the *real* world unless you were Dev who would use it as a tool to attract girls for a date? Psycho really!

I completely hated the idea of spending hours scrolling through the pictures of my friends or maybe friends' friends who are complete strangers to me vacationing and ostentatiously displaying it on their profile. What was the idea behind it?

Had to be show off, I presumed. How would other people know how much fun one is having or maybe it was an attempt to make their friends jealous of their merrymaking trips. I didn't see any other explicable reason behind it.

Weird right!

Wrong.

Well at least for the last few months.

Until about a couple of months before all three of us were like the 1.2 billion people of this country grumbling, complaining and criticizing every aspect of this country where we were born. It never occurred to us that we were also part of the reason behind all the mess in the country. We all loved American culture, their music, movies, lifestyle and everything about them. In short, like everybody else we hated being an Indian.

But who were we kidding?

Life can be a bitch if you treat her like one. I can still remember the date correctly - 19th of July. It was a day which wreaked havoc in our lives. A day that changed us forever!

I still remember the incessant moaning and weeping of Nikita, and Dev as well. I was completely paralyzed with shock. Surely, we had never expected such a thing to happen to us. But life has its own way of dealing with things. We learnt that the hard way.

We made a resolution that day. The idea was pretty simple – if you want to live in a better world, change it. But change always begins at home. Like is famously quoted by Mahatma Gandhi – "Be the change you want to see in the world."

Well, almost a year into the resolution now and I can proudly say for sure we did become that change and "yes it does work."

1

'NOT THAT IT MATTERED'

One Year Earlier.....

"Hey I love him," shrieked Nikita, referring to 'Joey' - the most loved character of the American hit series 'Friends.'

"He's definitely the best among the six of them."

I hated that about Nikita; she could howl and yell all day, very unhealthy for my ears. Though every other thing about her I appreciated. She was tall and healthy (she hated me when I refer to her as one) and was definitely 'bottom heavy'. Her heaviness in that particular area was further accentuated by the fact that she always wore tight jeans. Quite an effort it always took for me and Dev to keep our eyes away from that. She had fair and exceptionally flawless skin. Dev and I loved the fact that our best friend was 'hot'. She had thin black hair so long that it did manage to shroud a part of her hips and we hated it. She had hazel eyes with long, curved eyelashes that she was very proud of. I always fail to understand what was the big deal about that? *Girls!*

"No! Definitely not! Didn't I tell you Ross is the best?" Dev hooted, "Come on, he emotes so well and he is so damn hilarious."

I always thought I needed ear plugs when I was with them. It was always a competition between the two of them as to who would have the last laugh.

Dev was also tall, somewhere around six feet and had a good muscular frame with broad shoulders, thanks to his penchant for exercising. He religiously worked in the gym for atleast an hour everyday. I always thought he was over obsessed with it. The walls of his room were adorned by atleast a dozen posters of 'weird men posing only in their underwears' showing off their huge muscles with protruding nerves. I had no clue how was it helping them? Their hideous faces with clenched teeth wore the expression as if they needed to see the loo immediately. What a waste of life!

Then ofcourse there was the ubiquitous Salman Khan's poster though he was only shirtless as he always is, showing off his aesthetic six pack abs. He had always been Dev's idol and half his pictures on his facebook account belonged to the actor. What was worse was the fact that Dev had replicated poses by 'the weird men in underwears' and had posted them on his account for others to see and appreciate his body. Good heavens, atleast he wore his pants in them otherwise it would have been a traumatic sight for the viewers. He had made sure every inch of his body above the waist was scrupulously captured and displayed. I almost vomited the first time when I saw it. But he always told me that attracted a lot of girls to him. *Really!*

Well, the world can never be done away with weirdoes.

"What say Harsh?" Nikita looked upto me for confirmation.

I hated that, every time I was to resolve their crappy, petty spats. They loved arguing with each other whether or not it made any sense. Guys come on, enjoy the series, I wanted to tell them.

"Fuck you both," I however said. I was in the least mood for a discussion. I had just come back from my ship and was reveling in my vacation.

I am a sailor and sail on the high seas all the time, if I am lucky I do get a chance to see countries that my ship visits. Though it is so hectic in ports that a good night sleep is sometimes as good as a shore leave! After school, I had no qualms that I wanted to join merchant navy owing to the high paying salary and sightseeing of the world. The latter however, I learnt later, was an absolute misconception. Nevertheless, I was quite content with my profession, I mean who wants to slog his ass all day and night working in India to earn peanuts. Moreover I wanted to move out of India, there is too much of a struggle here and I always believed the quality of life was miserable.

Nearly a decade into this profession now and I have reached the peak of my career – a ship captain. It feels good, really good to command a massive ship in the gargantuan oceans of the world. I was however looking for an anchor – a girl to steady my life, just the way an anchor does to my ship. Well, to be frank, my mother was more interested in that than myself. She perpetually made it a point to remind me of my age in all her discussions.

"Look at you Harsh, you are already twenty eight, you need to get a girl for yourself and soon," she reiterated.

"Fine mom, look at Dev and Nikita, they are bachelors too." I could never think of a better excuse than that.

"They will eventually end up with each other, what would you do, huh?"

"What? No way" I resented, "that can't be true."

"Really," my mother looked intrigued, "so who do you think is with her when you are sailing?"

"They are just friends, like me and her." I almost yelled in disagreement.

"Okay," she shrugged and left my room. My mother could not think of a better discussion on the very first day of my leave at home. I could see what she was doing, trying to make me jealous so that I propose her. But I never thought about Nikita that way. Sure she was a wonderful person and a great friend, but it always felt a bit weird. Still I had to find someone and marry eventually. I didn't have many choices though, maybe Nikita. Was my mother right? I knew she was fond of her too and both were in complete sync with each other as her mother and mine were great friends too. I couldn't help thinking about her. Actually the problem was that I had never been with any other girl since school. My heart always skipped a beat when I thought about her. I knew she wasn't interested; not that she didn't like me or anything, but she had other plans with her life. And I never existed in any of her plans. I somehow never cared too much about it. Perhaps we were better off being friends.

All three of us had been friends since the last fifteen years now right since our school days. I decided to join navy and Dev and Nikita joined college – Sri Venkateshwara college near Dhaula Kuan in Delhi. They did a bachelor of commerce course *together* for 3 years. That always pierced my heart when I used to be lost and aloof on my ship. It somehow brought them closer to each other. Not that it mattered to me, but I always trusted Dev to screw it up with her.

And he did. On her 20th birthday he asked her out and Nikita had the typical answer ready. "Come on Dev we are just friends, aren't we?"

"Sure," he had replied.

Ha! I so loved it. Not that it would have mattered to me had she said yes and they would have dated each other, but I did believe that our friendship would have got affected. Priorities would have changed and suddenly I would end up being alone. Other than that the flirt that Dev was, it would have definitely led to their break up eventually and our little friend circle would have split. Glad that did not happen.

Life can be a wonderful experience if one has wonderful friends. I surely had the best of buddies in Dev and Nikita. Even while I was on the ship, I couldn't stop myself from thinking about them and the marvelous times we had spent together. I remember when we were in school we had taken an oath that no matter what happens we will grow old together and die infront of each other. Funny as it sounds, a decade had passed with us being together. But a lot had changed since then. I had made an irrevocable decision of joining the navy after school, which I did. Dev, although had joined college, but was not really a part of it! His father had a successful car business up and running for him. Nikita joined Evalueserve – a research company in Gurgaon as a business analyst. I had serious doubts about what she really did; her post was some serious business jargon I could never fathom. Nonetheless she was pretty happy with it.

With our careers in three different directions, it sure led to a bit of distance between us, but our love for each other always managed to bring us together atleast once every week. Sundays were always spent at Dev's place and there was absolutely no excuse allowed to skip it. His bungalow was in J-block market of Saket in Delhi near the crowd bustling market. His place was perfect for our rendezvous as it was at a stone throw distance from the huge and opulent Select Citywalk mall. Apart from that, the malls of Vasant Kunj were not far either. We were mall rats and could spend hours hanging around in them.

My home was in Lajpat Nagar in the southern most part of Delhi, a place where people all over the city flocked in its crowded and tacky Central Market area. It attracted a lot of people as the one thing we Indians inherently specialized in was customary in this part of the world – bargaining. All sorts of shrieks, yelling, howling was a characteristic of this place and one had to serpentine his way through the crowd to survive. But the one reason I loved being in this place was that every Sunday I got a chance to pick up Nikita from her home in Malviya Nagar – the centre of mine and Dev's place. It was always a wonderful 15 minutes drive from her place to Dev's and my only chance to spend time with her alone. Not that it mattered had Dev also been with us that time, but it wouldn't have been as good as my solitary time with Nikita. I used to share all sort of memories with her – both old and new and make her laugh. She had one of the coolest laughs in the world somewhat synonymous with a gleeful melody. It felt great even though we were good friends.

"Alright guys I'm out of here," said Nikita tucking her strands of hair behind her aesthetic ears. Her hair was really soft and pretty, golden brown in colour and I always loved that sight.

"Where to?" I inquired. I never wanted to be away from her. Not that I loved her but it was always good to be around a pretty girl, especially when she was your best friend.

"Home, where else Harsh, it's already eight," she yawned.

"You want me to drop you," I asked. I had never been too fond of driving but with only Nikita around in my car it felt good.

"No buddy thanks, my dad is also here, see you guys later."

She hugged us one by one. What I never understood was why she always did that to Dev first. Maybe he was closer to her. Not that it mattered to me, but I was always a bit curious about that. *Why always?*

I shrugged.

She held her bag around her arms, 'GUESS'- it said in big, block letters embedded on a shiny triangular metallic plate attached to the light brown coloured bag. I had bought it for her from the Changi airport of Singapore after I signed off from my ship this time. She had given me a good one minute tight hug at the Delhi airport when she along with Dev had come to pick me up. I was meeting her after four months but it had felt like a lifetime without her. I really loved the fact that never in the last ten years had Nikita failed to make it to the airport to pick me up. And of course Dev as well! I had missed him too.

"Bye Nikita," I said almost in reflex as my eyes were fixated at her until she was finally gone.

I turned around to face Dev. He was smiling contemptuously at me.

"What?" I said.

"What's with you dude, are you in love with her?" he scoffed.

"No way, ofcourse not," I replied. I was sure of that, I can't be in love with Nikita, she is my best friend.

"You sure, because it doesn't look like," he said again, almost mocking at me.

"No way Dev, she's a good friend, that's all." I replied casually.

"Okay, just curious." That fucking grin didn't leave his face the entire evening.

I thought about Nikita, she was very beautiful and adorable, it always felt great hanging around with her but I never had any sort of feelings for her. Or did I?

Maybe it was my solitude on my sailing days that could have changed my feelings for her. But it felt nothing; sure it gave me immense pleasure looking through her deep, penetrating eyes, watching her chuckle which led to dimples forming on the left side of her cheeks, listening to her, watching her sometimes puerile acts. But that was it. Or maybe as my mother talks about – the age factor, when you are in your late twenties you do need a life partner to settle around with. Whatever it was, it never mattered much to me. I always told myself "we are just friends" and got away with any of such thoughts. But still somewhere within me something had changed. I wanted to say something or may be hear something or maybe both. What was it that was bothering me from the last couple of months?

Was I in love with her? Not that it mattered.

Well, actually it did.

2

"NO COMMISSION CHARGED"

CARS are one of the coolest possessions of man. Recently I had decided to change my Hyundai i-10 as I had been really bored with it after driving it for over 3 years. I was planning to buy a new car as the superfluous money earned through my hard earned job was somewhat dripping out of my pockets. I had not made my mind as there were a lot of choices in the market and many new options pouring every month.

But Dev, my second best friend had been pestering me from the last couple of weeks to buy a second hand car from his shop rather than spending money on a new one.

"Dude think of it as this way, you will spend less than half money on an old car and you would still take home a car of a higher segment than a new one," he persuaded me like a minnow salesman.

I had my doubts about that, come on cars are a sign of status symbol in this country or atleast in this city. *What would my neighbours think? What would my batch mates think?*

I finally decided to end my dilemma by taking Nikita's opinion; after all, I thought she had an equal right on *our* car.

"Come on Harsh, how could you think of buying an old car?" Nikita instigated me, "Dev is a business man, you know that."

"Yeah Nikita alright, but I will spend half the money on an old car and would still take......" I tried repeating Dev's line but Nikita interrupted me in between.

"I won't sit in your car, who knows which dirty ass had been rubbing itself off on the seats."

"Ha, ha..." I laughed.

"Seriously Harsh, you are buying a new car, after all it would be my car as well."

What? Her last words hit me like a pleasant storm, *wow so she thinks likewise.*

Period! Dilemma over!

Still I made a visit to Dev's shop as he badgered me into atleast having a cursory look at the options he presented. Besides it didn't matter much to me as his shop was also in Central market, Lajpat Nagar – a five minutes walk from my place.

I reached his place in the morning to avoid the evening chaos that engulfed this market. I allowed myself a smile on reading his board. It said unabashedly in big, bold letters:

NAGPAL MOTORS

BUY/ SELL/ RENT CARS

NO COMMISSION CHARGED

What crap! Dev did not own all the cars in his shop barring a few, he had told me once as it would be very risky otherwise. He merely acted as an agent on behalf of the owner to sell their cars, so if they were not charging any commission, how the fuck were they even running this place, let alone making profits. I girded myself for an unpleasant morning.

The massive area covered by his shop was unlike the others in this place, some of them so miniscule, smaller than the smallest bathrooms I had seen in my life. It gave the owner absolutely no place to stand; sitting would have been a luxury. I wondered what made these people lead such a spartan life, living in such a claustrophobic area with the air filled with dust and sweat. Life was difficult here and I could make out by the incessant yelling of the shop owners to lure the people passing by offering them all sort of discounts to make them interested.

But Dev's place was different. Infront of his ship lay a stretch of land boasting of more than a dozen cars waiting to be driven by their prospective customers. The one thing common amongst all these cars was they all looked immaculately clean that belied their age. Only Dev or his father was privy to the fact that how many of them actually worked. I could see this was definitely a profitable business and why Dev gave two hoots of studying further or working elsewhere.

The office of Nagpal motors, however, was a very humble one; just about enough place for three people to sit. It did have an air-conditioner to combat the heat, but its purpose was defeated as it was seldom switched on owing to the frugal attitude of the Nagpal family. A lone tiny fan gyrated above producing wisps of fresh air that filled the room. The sound generated always won the contest from the air produced.

I hugged Dev after entering his office and greeted his father who was busy counting notes. He gave me a look of scorn and skepticism looking through his dark rimmed glasses before shaking his head. Dev ushered me outside of the room.

"Glad you decided to come," said Dev.

"Ah come on, you know I would have come," I replied. "So what's with the sign board, huh?"

"What?" Dev asked, unperturbed.

"No commission charged, really," I let out an uncharacteristic shriek. "I guess that wasn't there last time."

"Ah that, yeah, it's only to fool the customers, how would we earn profits otherwise?"

"I thought as much," I replied.

"Come," he signaled towards his cars. "I'll show you a lot of options."

I meekly followed him not in the least mood to have a look. I remembered Nikita's words

'After all it would be my car as well'. It gave me unprecedented happiness. There is something about love; I had read somewhere that it is the richest source of happiness. It surely was. So I had come to the stage where I finally conceded that 'yes I am in love and with Nikita'. I had already planned how I would break the ice with Nikita regarding 'our new relationship'. I would keep it simple though, I had thought. In my new car I would first take her on a long drive maybe on the wide and unblemished roads of the National Highway-8 connecting Delhi to Gurgaon. Maybe dinner at a good restaurant and dropping a ring in her champagne glass, like is done in many of the movies I had seen. How lame it was, I used to previously think, but now it appeared to me as the coolest ways of proposal. Obviously she would say yes and then come towards me for a hug. And then another cool thing would follow, I would hire a choir to play soothing music in the background. 'Wow,' she would scream and then hug me again. It felt awesome, never in the last twenty eight years of my life had I felt so complete and gratified.

"See Harsh, this Civic only 4 years old," Dev said.

"Harsh," Dev said again, this time shaking me, "hello, where are you lost?"

"Hmm," I woke up from my reverie, "nowhere, tell me?" I hated to traverse back in the real world. How I wish people could live in their dreams.

"See this car, driven by an army officer, only 18,000 kilometers." Dev tried cajoling me, "you know how well these people drive their cars, don't you?"

"Yeah, right," I said, a part of me was still not listening.

"Now my dad will give this car to you only for 7 lakhs, you won't even get a Honda City for that much." He was shaking his head trying to impress me, trying to prove how generous his father was. "See the difference dude, didn't I tell you?"

"Yeah, well, you did me tell me that."

"Okay, you don't look interested, I'll show you more."

Over the next hour he showed me all his cars and gave me many other options. A two year old Octavia, few years old City, SX4, Corolla, Sonata and all other brands that I was aware of. Seriously he did manage to convince me, if it was not for Nikita I would have definitely bought one. Dev was a wonderful person and a great friend, but when it came down to business, he was more devious than his father. He was so full of guile that even me, his best friend couldn't trust him.

Few meters away, we could hear his father and another elderly gentleman ranting at each other. He appeared to be one of their old customers and was pointing towards his car. Perhaps it was bought through Nagpal motors' services. Dev recognized him.

"Oh that crappy old man again," he muttered.

"Which man?" I asked, curious.

"That guy, he had purchased a car from us more than two months back but still comes here when his car gives him a trouble."

"So, why wouldn't he? Isn't he supposed to do that?"

Dev gave me a baleful look, "no, of course not, it's been more than a month now, we can't take a guarantee for so long, it wasn't our car anyway, although ummm....."

"What?" I asked, still curious.

"It's just that we got it revamped in such a brilliant way that it didn't appear old," he said with a shade of penitence.

"So how old was it?"

"12 years."

"And how old did you claim it was?"

"5 years."

"Ha," I laughed, "you asshole." We high fived, although sure it wasn't an appropriate time for it. "So no wonder, this guy is pissed."

"Hey I told dad, just tell him 8 years, but he insisted, what was I supposed to do."

I just looked at him and shook my head.

"You know what, dad even got the meter adjusted, from more than a lakh kilometers he got it down to forty thousand."

And we high fived again! Phew!

"You cheat fuckers." I said.

"Dude, this is India, here everyone is a cheat," he claimed, "you can't make money otherwise." The shade of guilt that he had, evaporated, and gave way to a sense of pride.

"Not true Dev, not everyone," I replied, "you can't judge the entire country by the action of a few people."

"Not few," he corrected, "all, okay to be fair almost all; you agree?"

I thought for a while, "I don't know, who are we to decide this?"

"It's true Harsh, believe it or not, go around this market, somewhere or the other some deceit is there in every shop."

"Right, so that justifies what you guys do."

"No I'm not saying it justifies," Dev countered, "but this is the way India is, you have to learn to live the unethical way."

"Alright, let it be Dev, screw it."

Maybe he was right. I didn't seem to care; I never lived in India much anyway, thanks to my job. I was myself not a big India fan; every day you pick up a newspaper or watch news on television, all one could see was scams everywhere. Everyone was trying to loot the country, maybe we were better off with Britishers ruling us, even if they looted us, atleast they were interested in our country's development. I guess Dev was right, in a country where majority of politicians seem to be corrupt, what difference does it make if we, the common man, were equally corrupt? Besides nobody gives a shit anyway, the law and order seems equally worthless. I don't know what made me think of our dear country, maybe it was an aftermath of a latest scam I had read. *What a waste of time!*

"So, which car do you want to buy?" Dev asked; he still believed I was buying a car from him. I showed him my middle finger.

"No seriously Harsh, consider buying the Civic I showed you first, it's done only 18000 kilometers."

"Really," I gave him a look of disdain, "go ask your dad first."

"No really," he said.

"Oh come on Dev and you want me to trust that."

"Yes," he replied. And what he said after that made me kick his butt so bad that he sat on the floor for the next two minutes. "Take it dude, no commission charged, really."

"What?" *Bang!*

"Oh fuck, that hurt you bastard."

"I can't believe it Dev that you are doing this to me as well." I said after he appeared to be over the pain.

"Do what?" He said gently massaging his butt. The pain didn't seem to fade away.

"That Civic is not yours right?" I said pointing towards the metallic blue car. He said it was 4 years old, but I had serious doubts now. "Then how could you possibly sell it to me without any commission."

"No seriously take it."

"Fuck," I exclaimed. "I thought I was your best friend."

"Of course you are my best friend."

"Still you are doing this to me, fooling me like your other customers."

"Okay fine, you give me six and a half lakhs only, fine."

"Fuck you Dev, I'm never going to see you in your shop again, you are a horrible person here." I said and turned around to leave. Just then his father came running to me; he had probably been eavesdropping on our conversation. He called out my name from behind. I was in the least mood to strike a conversation with him. Even on Sundays at his home, me and Nikita never spoke to him much. I didn't know what he wanted to say now, maybe his curt behaviour with me in his office was disturbing him and he wanted to make up for that. I prepared myself for an unpleasant conversation.

But no, it wasn't about that.

"Take it son," he said sheepishly, "no commission charged."

I ran.

3

FACEBOOK.COM

THE next Sunday as is always the case, I and Nikita went over to Dev's home. It was a very pleasant ride after I picked up Nikita. I drove slowly at the bare minimum so I could maximize my time spent with her. Normally I used to hate the hideous Delhi traffic abusing it relentlessly, but today it seemed awesome. I absolutely loved it when the cars behind me were honking at me with no real reason trying to overtake me and I submitted to them in gaiety. I also loved when cars in front reduced their speed at the last minute without any indication only to learn later they planned to take a u-turn that was not allowed, clearly ordered by Delhi Traffic police by their conspicuous "U-turn not allowed" sign. What was even better was the fact that when I wanted to take a left turn to enter Saket coming from Malviya Nagar, the free left was obstructed like it always was by the people who wanted to go straight. Well it would certainly save them a minute or two as opposed to waiting behind the traffic that went straight, so clearly it made sense. *Motherfuckers!* I lost a

21

solid five minutes that way as I had to wait for the signal to become green for the traffic that had to go straight. Well, the free left was not free anymore; guess we Indians don't like anything for free.

Then there were these ubiquitous auto rickshaws and cycles coming in and out from all sides of the roads that forced me to press the breaks of my car more than the accelerator. Not to forget the brave pedestrians who never gave a damn about the zebra crossing or traffic signals while darting in and out and crossing roads, sometimes just walking leisurely as if in a garden, expecting the cars to stop before them. And then of course, the occasional cow that had been abandoned and had nowhere to go. I almost banged into her when she suddenly veered left into me causing the traffic behind to stop and abuse me. "Oye behenchod what is this, blind or what?"

I so loved it, completely appreciated the traffic sense and patience of our people. Maybe foreigners should learn from us how to help their fellow citizen to spend solitary time with the girl he loved.

When we reached Dev's place, I scouted his house.

"What are you looking for Harsh?" Dev said, looking up through his laptop.

"Nothing, is your father home?"

"No, why, you got some work with him?"

Thank god; work! Are you kidding me? He would have definitely been pissed at me for my irreverence to his advice a few days back at his shop where I chose to run rather than listening to him.

"No, just curious," I replied looking at his screen to see what kept him busy.

It was facebook.com. Dev had this knack of enticing women online through his disguised professional abilities. To some he was a doctor, to some a national level hockey player, others thought of him as an air force pilot, a ship captain, an assistant director, owner of a modeling agency and many others. His profession changed depending on the intellect of the woman he interacted or her needs. Seldom, he used to manage a date with them and that's what kept him going. I remember him dating a bimbo whom he had promised to get a break in the modeling world. Poor girl got married a couple of weeks later when her parents didn't approve of her aspirations. Dev was shattered that day as all his efforts bore no fruits. Nevertheless he was dejected but never out of focus. Next he had become an air force pilot.

I scrolled through his chat window to see what he had become today. I and Nikita laughed in unison when he had fooled the girl to believe that he was a space scientist.

"Dev are you crazy?" Nikita laughed hysterically, "how can you be a space scientist, you sell cars." I and her high-fived! Wow, it felt great; her soft hands against mine.

"So why not huh," Dev shrugged, "what I am to do if she's so passionate about science fiction movies, that's my only chance of cracking her."

"Ha, ha, ha," the hysteria continued.

Seriously, I thought, from where does Dev get these crazy ideas? In a way it was good for me – Dev's flirtatious nature. It made Nikita distant from him; my mother would not be aware of this but there was definitely and could be nothing between them. *Thanks Dev, I would always be obliged.* I loved him even more for this. Now Nikita had nowhere to go, we were the only guy friends she ever hung around with. Sure she did have some male colleagues in her office, but she was never in such great terms with them as she was with us. I stood a great chance of having her all by myself; my best competitor was busy fiddling with his keyboard trying to impress the *sci-fi girl* and fixing a date with her. Maybe time had come for me to put forth my feelings for Nikita. I was waiting for the best time to do it but I also wanted to take Dev by my side. He was the one who was better at girls; I had absolutely no clue how to deal with them. He would definitely give me a better idea how to win her over, I thought. Besides he was privy to almost everything in my life then why not this.

"Done," Dev said as he logged out of his account. He appeared victorious.

"Done what?" Nikita asked; I was about the say the same thing a second later. *Wow so we do connect well.*

"Tomorrow at nine is our date, now got to do some research what these guys at ISRO do." Dev said opening google.com.

"You want me to help you with something." I asked coyly.

"Go help yourself dude," Dev dismissed, "what sort of a guy doesn't even have a facebook account these days?"

"My sort of a guy," I replied. "So why do I need a facebook account anyway when I have my best friends with me all the time."

"Dude we'll video chat," the lamest thing he could have ever said, I thought. We were right there in front of each other, why the fuck should we *video chat*. The internet mania was beyond me.

"No Harsh, Dev is right, at least have an account may be you can get in touch with all your friends." Nikita said.

"You guys are my friends, all my friends." I replied, a profession like mine didn't offer a good friend circle. But that was okay I didn't need any other friends anyway, besides one has to lose something in order to gain something in life. Not sure really what I was losing here or for that matter gaining. Nevertheless I was having a good time in my life and it was going to get all the more better as Nikita would be a part of it soon. I didn't need a computer or some freaky social website to get me all that. But Dev as adamant as he always is again logged back to facebook.com and clicked on "Sign up". I looked below "it's free and will always be". *Damn it!* It's free, I thought then why not, it's anyway a win - win situation for me. I gave my e-mail id and within minutes Dev created my account. Ha! It was that simple; I always thought of it as some sort of a puzzle that vexed me and I would have never done that alone. I guess I was a bit philistine in this particular area. Within the next minute, both logged back to their respective accounts and then logged me back. I could see the number 2 on top left hand side of my profile page.

"What's that?" I asked pointing towards the tiny little number.

"You got 2 friend requests." Dev said, "that's me and Nikita."

And there it was, my two best friends in my apparent world. I was sure I would never be using my account.

I was completely wrong.

✻ ✻ ✻ ✻

Two days later I got a call from Dev, a much unexpected one at nine in the morning as Dev was not a morning person. His job or business as he refers to (though a car dealer wouldn't qualify as a businessman) didn't require him to see the morning sun. It was about the sci-fi chic. I was baffled.

"Dude what is happening to me?" he said in a tone that appeared slightly concerned.

"What?" I said with a shade of asperity as I rubbed by eyes. I wasn't a morning person either.

"This is the second time in the last month." He continued, still in a worried tone.

"What Dev?" I said, too tired to talk, "stop your bloody riddles, come to the point."

"That sci-fi chic is also getting married."

"What?" Now that was funny, I almost laughed my way into his misery.

"You got a Midas touch Dev, any girl you get into gets married," I said, "maybe you should consider setting up a matrimonial service, it'll do good business. Well at least it will save you from cheating customers at your stupid car shop."

"Yeah right," he exclaimed. "I almost thought it could have gone somewhere after our date."

"Fuck you Dev, you'll find another one, there are plenty of fishes in the water." I said.

"Alright," said he, "so when do you plan proposing Nikita?"

So he was aware, well you can't really hide things from your friends, can you?

"How do you know I was going to do that?" I asked casually.

"I know you love her the way you look at her."

"Really," I asked, not sure if my gaze at her was too obvious.

"Harsh, don't waste any time; just do it."

Just do it, I thought as much. I don't know what was cooking with Nikita these days, though I was sure she was single or else she would have definitely told one of us. I was still not sure how would I initiate the talk. It was scary; I did have goose bumps when I thought about doing it. But there was no escaping from the most important thing of my life.

"Right Dev, I'm doing it today."

"Wow, really," Dev said. I was so happy he was excited for me.

"Really," I said as I hung up the phone. Time has come, I thought.

I looked up at the watch and dialed Nikita's number.

4

THE PROPOSAL???

THE Select Citywalk is the most prolific mall that our city has seen over the years. Flanked by MGF Metropolitan and DLF mall on its either side, the three of them stand right in the heart of the southern part of this city sharing few acres of land among them.

We had been frequent visitors to this place ever since its inception in October 2007. The three malls boast of all the world class brands from around the world facilitating shopping that could be done under one roof.

Today, however only me and Nikita had made a visit, Dev being a bit unwell. I loved the way he feigned illness on the phone when we three were on a conference call earlier this morning.

"What happened Dev, you okay?" asked Nikita when he apologized for not meeting us.

"Yeah just a bit of fever," he coughed, "you guys carry on." I so loved him for that. Only the two of us meant a certain proposal by me today, Dev had planned that in advance. I did a bit of rehearsals in the morning before picking her up from her place. It was definitely on. I even told my mother about my plans for the day. It excited her too, something she had been pestering me to do ever since I came back.

"Alright mom, I'll do it for you." I had said hiding personal reasons.

"Wow, love you son," she said hugging me, with a tear drop off her eyes. Too dramatic, I thought. *Indian mothers!* She had no clue how much I loved Nikita, there wasn't any need actually to tell her, unless she said no. However, I never expected that answer. *Why would she reject me?* I couldn't see a plausible reason for that.

We sat at 'Gloria Jeans's coffees', the Australian coffee giant. Nikita flipped through the menu card as my mind worked with an agility that even I was unaware of. I thought of the various options to crack a conversation. Guess the rehearsals at home were a complete waste of time as I was irretrievably tongue tied in front of her. I saw couples around cozying with each other and the place was definitely redolent with all the romance one could crave for. Love was in the air and I could feel it.

A large LCD television peered at us from above the wall adjoining ours. A prominent news channel hollered about Anna Hazare and his fast unto death campaign. It spoke about the credentials of the man and how history preceded his morality, his struggle in Maharashtra a few years ago to construct a model village and how it had made him earn the reputed Padma Bhushan award in 1992. The primary purpose of this movement was to alleviate corruption in our country through a Jan Lokpal bill.

"What do you have to say about that?" Nikita asked, pointing towards the screen.

"All I can say is the guy has balls." I replied, "I mean how often you see a single man standing up and fighting the system? He reminds me of Mahatma Gandhi."

"Oh really," said Nikita with a raised brow, "were you even born then?"

"Well we all have studied about him, that's exactly what he did isn't it?"

"Yeah, but that was him; I don't know what this guy is upto," she shrugged. "What change can he bring in this stupid country now?"

"Don't be such a cynic Nikita, all big revolutions are initiated by a single man first, and then the entire country comes together."

"Really," she raised her brow again; I don't know why she kept saying that word. What if she says that when I say 'Hey I love you'. God, I'll be so doomed.

"So tell me Harsh, which other great men you know who started such revolution single-handedly."

Why the hell was she taking my history lessons? What the fuck was happening, was this a history class? And I thought I was here to propose her. I scratched my head to answer her question first.

"Martin Luther king junior," I said a bit unsure of that.

"Okay, and," she wanted more.

"Mahatma Gandhi," I replied sheepishly.

"That's already done." She dismissed.

I scratched my head again. I have always been bad at history in school and Nikita was aware of it. "Abraham Lincoln, maybe" I said skeptically.

"Ha!" she laughed, "crap."

"Okay, Nikita why are we talking about this, let's talk about something else." I was waiting for *my something else.*

"Alright," she said, "let it be, but this fast unto death campaign has no meaning, call me cynical or whatever but really this isn't going anywhere."

I don't know what was wrong with us Indians, instead of appreciating someone's unconditional efforts, we somehow always found a reason for criticism. Well, I didn't know where his campaign was headed and frankly didn't seem to care anyway, but I never doubted the man's credibility. At the age of seventy three, he was too charged up for bringing about a change in this country. Though he did have the support of the respected Kiran Bedi and the social activist Arvind Kejriwal, still somewhere I thought of him as a modern day Gandhi. Today, these guys were at Jantar Mantar, a prominent historic place in Delhi where Hazare pledges to fast unto death if the government does not accept the draft prepared by the civil society group for the Lokpal Bill which would look into the corruption charges against our ministers. The news spoke about how people kept pouring in huge numbers for support of the campaign and how from day one the government was under constant pressure to accept his demands.

"Hey what say Nikita, you want to go there tomorrow?" I asked intrigued by the news. The news reporters are somewhat better than a sales person, they so convince you with their information that even I got a bit enthusiastic about it. I didn't know when my proposal was coming.

"Are you crazy Harsh?" she replied, shunning my enthusiasm, "nothing is going to happen, this is absolute crap. I guess the media has created too much hype about it like it always does just to sell their news. I have got more important things to take care of than support this stupid campaign."

"Yeah, actually you are right, even I got more important things to do."

I don't why but somehow I felt like a loser. I mean we complain about our country all the time and when someone stands up to fight, we can't find time. The least we could have done was to support him.

"I don't know Nikita but we are corrupt too in our own ways, I mean what have we done to improve things in our country apart from our consistent grumbling?"

"Well it's not our job to improve the system, what are these politicians for?" She sort of yelled. She always had to win an argument.

She was right, but I didn't even remember the last time I had taken part in voting during elections. I was too lazy for that. "Hey when was the last time you voted?" I asked Nikita. Maybe she was even lazier.

"Me, never; whom can you vote, all of them are corrupt anyway," she replied nonchalantly.

I smiled. "You know Nikita, sometimes I feel we don't even have the right to complain about the mess in our country, we don't even find time to cast a vote."

She fell silent. "I don't know, maybe you are right," Nikita finally did agree, "but I guess that's because we know there isn't any point anyway."

I kept quiet; I didn't know why we were even talking about it. I told the waiter to change the channel; the news about Hazare won't stop for a month atleast. *God bless him and help him too, hope he succeeds in whatever he has strived for.* Well, that definitely was the least I could have done.

I looked at Nikita who was busy gorging on her club sandwich. Her long untied hair fell on her food, which she brushed aside by her spidery fingers. The black nail polish and colourful bracelets entwined around her fair arms almost made me skip a bit when I noticed them a bit too closely. It was always a phenomenal sight. In between, the cheese of her sandwich found its way to her lips which she neat fully wiped through her tongue. God, I badly wanted to kiss her. I thought of saying it right now, but could not muster the strength. This was crazy, I had been with Nikita for so many years now, spoke about all sort of nonsense but had never been uncomfortable with her; today however there was this unprecedented anxiety and jitteriness that had completely taken over my soul. I felt a huge lump in my throat.

"You know it's funny," Nikita resumed criticizing the system, "when our prime minister talks about our group of ministers interacting with these social activists to form an effective Lokpal bullshit."

"What's funny about that?" I asked.

"Oh come on," Nikita said, "which minister is not corrupt and if someone's not, then he definitely keeps his eyes shut to all the filth around him. You can't fight corruption that way when everyone is a part of it."

That's it. I wasn't interested anymore in her philosophical take of our politics and corruption. This had to end now so I could talk about 'my stuff'. The clock was ticking and Nikita would talk about getting back to her home. She had been working from home since the last couple of weeks; hence she was out with me on a weekday. But working from home didn't guarantee peace as she found herself more occupied than she was at her office.

"You know what Harsh? I don't want to live in this country anymore." She sighed.

"What? You are kidding right." I asked with a tinge of curiosity.

"No really," she said in a serious and impassive expression, "in fact I have applied for an MBA in quite a few American universities and the day I get a call I'll be out of this shit."

"No way, what?" my curiosity had now reached its peak, "why didn't you tell us this before?"

"I'm still waiting for their confirmation for my admission; once it was through I would have told you guys."

"What are you doing Nikita, why are you leaving us?" I said, almost begging her. My proposal would obviously have no value if she was planning to leave India.

"Come on Harsh, I'm not leaving you guys, we are best friends. It's just that I don't want to live in this country anymore, I just hate being here."

"But why, it's great to be in your own country." I spoke in a non-committal tone. Truly, I myself hated being here. Given a choice even I would have left this country a long time back. The scams, scandals, traffic jams, population and pollution were not a thing I wanted to be associated with.

"I don' think so," she said shaking her head in disapproval. It seems she was hell-bent on leaving me. I had nothing to tell her now; my proposal would seem to be the lamest thing in the world. I decided keeping that to myself at least for the time being. First things first, I thought.

"But you do plan coming back after your MBA right?" I asked.

She didn't answer but was thinking, "maybe not, who knows I might land up in a job there, you know how much

I love America and their culture right, what if I find an American, it will be so cool I can be an American citizen if I get married to him."

"Yeah, right," I couldn't help putting forth a solemn expression. Maybe that would do the trick of making her realize my love for her. But it didn't. I don't know why but I felt blood rushing through my veins. *Did I love her that much?* I myself wasn't sure about that but nevertheless it ceased to matter now. I won't see her for years together, it felt weird. Maybe we could video chat on facebook, Dev was probably right. I guess he could foresee this.

"Let's go Harsh," she said pointing towards her watch, another of my gift to her from last year, "got some work to do."

"Alright."

All this while I always believed that I just adored her and probably she was good to get married to, but the very idea of she leaving India and me forever pierced my heart and made me realize that I loved her madly and irrevocably and without her my life would never be as awesome as it is when I am with her.

Something had to be done to convince her to stay back.

Little did I know an appalling incident just a few days later was the remedy to this in the most obnoxious way I could have ever imagined!

5

MY STUPID HEART!

I tossed up on my bed all night. I don't know why but a few tear drops did escape my eyes. I didn't like this feeling, it was terrible. How come I love her so much? Just last year I never felt like this. I had seen it in the movies, read in books about how good and bad life can get when someone falls in love. Unfortunately for me, love gave me the latter feeling. It felt horrible; just when I wanted to break the ice with her, she told me she was leaving. Couldn't she have told this to me before, heck I wouldn't have fallen in love with her for plausible reasons, but who knows this stupid love as we know works according to its own whims and fancies? We are just at the mercy of it.

I thought about the last evening and suddenly it dawned on me that I didn't even tell her that I was in love. Maybe that would have changed her mind. I guess I was stupid to just walk away without even telling how I felt for her. I looked at the time, it said 2:50.

Crap, what was I doing so late at night, why was I not sleeping? It was too late to call her; maybe I could gather the strength tomorrow morning and tell her how much I loved her. I guess that was my only resort if I wanted her to stay back. But I knew I have always been bad at expressing myself, it wasn't going to be an easy task. Still, it had to be done; love had not left me with any other choice. I tried massaging my chest to give some relief to my heart who wasn't in peace with itself, stupid moron was jumping up and down or maybe it was dilating and contracting too fast for my comfort. Relax buddy, I told him, there are plenty of fishes in the water. But it wasn't listening, I guess Dev's heart was much better than mine; this line definitely got him peace.

A lot of peace!

I tried sleeping, but my stupid heart did not allow my eyes to rest. What was the damn connection anyway? What was happening to me? This was definitely not cool. I looked at the watch again. 3:10. Damn it! I picked up my phone and dialed a number. No, not Nikita, I didn't have the balls. It was Dev.

"What?" Dev answered. I don't why but he sounded fresh, as though he was awake. Or maybe that was because I hadn't slept.

"You awake?" I asked; I knew I was in for a lot of abuses had it been otherwise.

"Yeah," he said, "what makes you call me so late?"

"Nikita," I replied, "but how come you are up, this time?"

"I met a very pretty girl at the gym two days back, new admission. She's so hot dude with stuff at the right places and her hair is so long you'll love it. Her skin is so soft and she a got a tattoo of a mermaid on her left arm. You know her eyes are like…"

That's it, I had to stop him. "Crap, I don't what her description at this time; it didn't answer my question anyway."

"Okay," He paused. "I am chatting with her on facebook."

"Oh god, not again." I wish I had a heart like him, it never fell in love. See you asshole, I pointed towards my heart, why can't you be like his.

"So who are you for her?"

"A captain."

"What? Why? Why have you taken my rank?"

"It's cool or atleast it sounds cool."

"No it is cool," I said. I missed my ship.

"Okay so why did you call?"

"Of course," I forgot talking about her; wish I could forget her like that forever. I don't want to be discussing girls with Dev at three in the morning. "I couldn't say it."

"Say what?"

"Dev fuck you man, you know what and can you please stop chatting with her; my stuff is more serious."

"Okay, okay just give me a minute, I'll finish with her and will call you back."

"Bye," I said as I hung up. He called after twelve and a half minutes.

"Yeah, tell me now."

"Nikita is leaving India," I said. I found that difficult to even speak.

"Really, why?"

"She wants to do her MBA from America."

"Really, why?"

Fuck, Dev can be irritating at times. "How do I know?"

"But there are good colleges in India as well, why go to America?"

"Exactly"

"But so what let her go, she'll come back right, it's not like she's going to another planet forever."

"Maybe she plans to settle there if she gets a job and you know how much she loves Americans, maybe she'll get married to one."

"Okay, now I know what you mean."

"Thank you; besides two years is a lot of time, what if she finds someone there, she doesn't even love me."

"Oh, well then at least tell her about your feelings, may be that would make her stop."

"Really," I said a bit skeptic.

"Yes Harsh, girls are very dumb; they will do anything for you if you tell them about your love. Trust me it's not difficult to fool girls, in fact it's very easy. You know when I was a fashion designer, I told this girl she had just the right fashion sense to become one too and then we started hanging out, things didn't work out between us as I had thought but when I was a doctor, this girl I met was so crazy about me, you know she even said that if it was...."

Fuck him, I stopped listening. I don't know what was wrong with me; I was taking Dev's advice on love. Something had to be terribly wrong with me.

It was; I was in love. I thought about speaking to my mother the next morning. She was definitely a sensible person.

"And when I told this girl that I play hockey at national level she was so impressed, it almost made her fall for me, but you know me don't you Harsh, I am so....".

God, he was still speaking, wonder if he even remembered what the topic was.

"Bye Dev, good night." I said and clicked my phone.

I waited for the morning.

❊ ❊ ❊ ❊

My mother got a cup of hot tea for me. I somewhat felt fresh, I didn't remember what happened after I hung up on Dev, maybe I fell asleep. *Thank god.*

"Mom do you miss dad?" I asked when she came back to my room to collect the empty cup. I was never too comfortable talking with my mother about her divorce, hell I never even discussed about my father with her. Guess something's are better unsaid.

"Why would you ask me that?" she said disinterestedly.

"Generally," I said.

She kept the cup aside and sat on the bed besides me. She took a deep breath and then looked towards me. "What is gone is gone; I don't care much about it now." There was a sort of hollowness in her voice which had understandably crept in. My father and mother were divorced more than fifteen years now but still she was not over him. I don't know what was wrong with him that he fell in love with another woman and left us just like that. It left deep scars on my mother's heart but she never let me feel those. I guess that was part of the reason, I had never been in any relationships. I always thought I would end up like my father. It also made me a bit of a reserved person that I was now. Maybe that was the reason I had difficulty in expressing my feelings.

"Don't worry son, you and Nikita will do pretty well together." She said after shunning her old memories.

"You think so?"

"Yeah sure," she said, "just go and tell her."

"She's leaving India to do her MBA, what's the point?"

"So then you must tell her now before she leaves."

"Or maybe I should never let her go in the first place."

"Whatever you do Harsh, just make sure few years later you don't regret not doing or saying something, regret is more painful than the actual pain, always remember that." She advised moving her hand over my hair.

Regret is more painful than the actual pain. It was true, won't let that happen to me, I thought.

"You want me to talk to her or maybe Suman," she said. It would have been so lame if my mother told Nikita's mother about it – the dumbest way of proposal ever. I am sure Nikita would kick my ass for that for the rest of our life.

"No ma, you don't need to do that, leave that to me."

"You'll manage?"

"Yeah I will." I replied. I had to fight my biggest fears, I thought. I hugged my mother and sauntered towards the washroom.

Time for some action!

6

LIKE FATHER, LIKE SON!!!

I did the dumbest thing in the world. After speaking to Dev last night and listening to his utter nonsense, I still did not learn. I went to Dev's place in the morning to take advice how to talk it out with Nikita. Maybe it was that I thought he hung out with a lot of women so he was comfortable talking to them or maybe I was being a complete idiot. Nevertheless, I had nothing to lose so I thought might as well give it a shot.

When I reached there, I went straight to his office as I saw his father outside ranting with another of his customer. Same old crap he must have done as last time, but what was it this time, maybe he had lied about its age or adjusted the meter or well who knows, the entire engine.

As I opened the door, Dev was shirtless and the miniscule office stank of his body odour. He had his legs up on the chair, head towards the floor and was counting 28, 29, 30... Pushups, god, this time of the day! I was so fed up of his madness for exercising. As he got up after 50 pushups, he was smiling.

"See I can do fifty, huh," he said proudly, "how much can you do?"

I shrugged my shoulders and slapped him. "Well I can do fifty of those!" I said.

"Why are you always hitting me? You see my muscles; I'll squeeze you to death if I want." He showed me his biceps after pumping them. All I saw was his clenched teeth.

"Okay, why are you exercising here?" I ignored his question.

"Oh well," he replied in an expression of pride with a wink at me, "you know me I'm going on a date with Neha."

"Who's Neha?" I had completely lost track of his girlfriends.

"You know her, last night I was chatting with her, the one I met at the gym."

"Ah okay, the girl for whom you stole my rank."

"Yeah, see you remember."

"No it's just that every time I meet you, you are with a different person and have a different profession." I said with a shrug of my shoulder.

"Oh insulting me, are you?" He drank a glass of water. "Anyway what brings you here early in the morning?"

"Dev it's already afternoon."

He looked at his watch. "Oh yeah it is, completely lost track of the time. So you want to have a look at a car. I got many new options since the last time you were here."

I felt like slapping him again. "Never mind, so I am going to pop up the question with Nikita," I said, ignoring him and not wasting any more time lest he get started with any of his other crappy talks.

"Good for you, just do it man." He said patting my arms.

"But tell me dude, how do I get started, it's so bloody unnerving."

"No it isn't, that's because you think it is."

Finally a sensible one from him, it is true, I have made my mind to think like that. Alright point noted.

"Come on look at me, I can ask out just about any girl that comes my way, it's that simple. I never feel nervous, besides you love her. What more can Nikita want?"

The door of his office opened as his father entered. It was a very unpleasant sight. He wore an angry expression that made his face a bright red. But immediately he turned it into a congenial one when he looked at me.

"Oh Harsh, after a long time huh," he said, "so what brings you here early in the morning?"

Like father, like son!

"Dad, it's already afternoon, where are you lost?" Dev replied. I controlled my urge of slapping him again.

"Oh yeah, so Dev did you show some cars to Harsh?" He asked Dev and then turned towards me, "son we have a lot of new options since the last time you were here."

What the fuck! Why was he repeating everything that Dev said?

"No uncle I am good really."

"No son, have a look," he insisted, "We have cars whose average does not exceed three years."

I looked at Dev who avoided my gaze. *Damn you guys!*

"Look son! All of them have done less than twenty thousand kilometers."

I looked at Dev again. He was outright embarrassed to say the least. I almost felt like laughing at the old man's face. Had he not been Dev's dad, I don't know what I would have done with him.

"Why don't you tell him Dev?" he asked his son, "he's a nice boy, we'll give him a good car."

"Yeah dad okay, I'll tell him." Dev replied, "We are actually in the middle of something important."

"Okay, I'll leave you young boys to it." His father said as he left us. I gave Dev a look of disapproval. Dev sighed. "Come on Harsh, he's too old to improve, let it go."

I did let it go, I had more important things to take care of. "So where were we?" I asked.

"Yeah, my dear Nikita," I replied, answering my own question.

"See dude, I guess your first priority should be to ensure she doesn't leave India. You never know what's going to happen there and then think about your other stuff. Just convince her not to do an MBA, you know, maybe you can tell her that you are earning enough for the both of us and she could just sit whole day and blow your money. Girls like this, you know when I told one of my old girl that I earn a lot of money and maybe I can buy her......"

"Stop, stop, stop that right away," I warned him immediately not to flow into his own futile stories as he always does. Until now he was talking sense, I could actually tell her that, I mean any girl would love the fact that his to be husband is earning enough.

"Yeah and I could probably tell her that take it easy, you are a woman you don't need to be so ambitious, I'm there for that."

"Yeah see, now you are talking."

"Or perhaps, why all the hard work when I'm there for that?"

"Cool, now you are getting it."

"Isn't it? And then maybe the ring and the million dollars question."

"Which question?" Dev was dumbfounded.

Slap! "Ouch! Why again? I was only kidding."

"Sorry."

I was glad I came here, Dev definitely made some sense. Perhaps first, I should as a friend dissuade her not to do an MBA. Perhaps I could tell her that it is a complete waste of a year or maybe two, and then she needed to mortgage her life for the next five years in order to pay the heavy loan she would have taken for her studies. An American MBA is outrageously expensive and definitely not worth its value. They make the entrance to their colleges so stringent that only the brightest students can get through. These students would have anyway done well with or without an MBA, and then these B-schools just take credit for their success. But what people don't realize is it was not the MBA but their own credibility that got them success in life.

This, I thought, I would tell Nikita. Besides she seems to forget that she's a girl, she doesn't need to be so career oriented, I am there for that.

And then the proposal, aha!

It all seemed crystal clear now, no doubts whatsoever.

Midway between my thoughts, I was interrupted by a call on my cell phone.

It was Nikita.

"Yeah baby," I replied.

"Hey, I don't even have a passport I just realized," she sounded worried, "you guys please come tomorrow with me to the passport office. I don't want to go through that shit of dealing with government officials alone; you know how nasty they are."

"So you still want to go to America, is it?"

"Yeah, of course."

"Alright, we'll see you tomorrow."

I looked at Dev who appeared inquisitive. "What happened?"

"Tomorrow," I said, "I'll propose to her at the passport office."

7

AAAATHHOOOOOOO….

SAME as always, I picked up Nikita from her place at Malviya Nagar. I wore my best clothes for the very important occasion. Fuck, it actually took me a good one hour to decide what to wear; terrible as it sounds, I had become a little girl myself. I sprayed perfume all over my body and styled my hair with oodles of gel. I had to look perfect. Love, as weird as it is, makes us do all sorts of crazy things. I used to never even wash my face before going out but love had changed me. I wasn't the same person anymore. My mother who stood behind me was a testament to this. She smiled all along and made me a bit embarrassed.

"Harsh! Are you getting married today?" she laughed, "look at you, you have gone completely crazy."

"Laugh mom as much as you want to, but today I'm going to do it."

"Okay, all the best. Make sure nothing stops you today." She said as she left me to do the final bit of touches to my hair. *Oh my god! What have I become?*

49

"Done," I said the fifth time in the last fifteen minutes looking at the mirror. But this time I was really done. I picked up my wallet and checked if I had enough cash maybe for a dinner at a five star hotel after Nikita said yes. I picked up the car keys and pranced towards the door.

"Right ma, bye, wish me luck."

"Bye, good luck." I heard a faint voice behind me as I ran towards my car.

When I was in my car, I thought of doing it right after I picked her up from her place. By the time we would have reached Dev's place, maybe we would be in each other's arms. What a nice surprise to give to Dev!

As she entered the car, she looked devastatingly hot. I felt a huge surge of blood through my veins as I gasped for breath. She looked stunning in her faded blue jeans that were torn at quite a few places exposing her beautiful legs. I somehow failed to understand the fashion behind it. The more the jeans were torn, the more expensive it got. Her white coloured top matched immaculately with the broken threads of her jeans. She always wore multicoloured bangles that beautified her arms. But the one thing that always caught my eyes was her long, untied hair. I think she had got them straightened recently as they appeared exceptionally neat and crisp. Their scent filled my car in a matter of seconds. I was so lost and completely blown over.

"Hey Harsh, you are looking so good, what's up?"

"Look who's talking," I said distracted by her. I didn't want her to be the reason for an accident.

"Ha!" she laughed, "so where to?" She almost ignored my little praise of her.

"Dev's place," I replied. I looked at my watch, it was definitely more than fifteen minutes for us before we reached, may be more if the Delhi traffic helped me as they always did. I girded myself.

"So Nikita," I began, "why do you want to an MBA?"

"Why would I not want to do an MBA?" she fired it back imperiously at me.

Not a good start!

"No I mean you are a girl, you don't need to be so career oriented."

"And what makes you think I shouldn't be career oriented." She fired it back again.

"No I mean you are a girl, you don't need to be so career oriented." I don't know why I repeated the same line.

"Harsh, come on we are not living in the twentieth century, women are equally focused in this era."

I had to get out of this mess.

"Yeah sure you are right," it was important to accord with her first if I wanted this conversation to go somewhere, "but don't you feel it is more important to get married to a good guy first, you know who has enough money and who could take care of you."

"Aha, since when did you start thinking like a girl, huh?" She began laughing and brushed my hair. I did love her hands against my hair but why did she have to spoil my hair style.

"So you agree right?"

"Yeah of course," she conceded, "which girl wants to slog her ass after marriage, but where the hell do you find these guys who are both – good and rich."

Here, right in this car!

"Well, look around, you'll find them." I said. I should have said 'me' instead. *Damn!*

"Where?" she said putting her hands above her eyes and turned everywhere except me.

It kind of annoyed me. *She didn't even consider me!* Ouch! That hurt.

"What about me?" My eyes were shut when I said that. That was scary.

"Oh Harsh you are sweet." She said pinching my cheeks. *Just sweet, what the fuck!*

"Just sweet," I don't know from where I got the strength to say that.

Her phone rang; she picked it up ignoring me. *Oh dear god, what was happening!*

It was Dev. He wanted to know how much more time for us to reach his place. *Perfect timing asshole!*

"Yeah sorry," she said "you were saying something."

Why do girls have such short memories?

I looked at the time again; it was about five minutes to reach. I guess it was pointless to talk about it now. "Never mind," I said, "later."

"Okay," she shrugged.

I looked at her through the front mirror which I had adjusted so I could have a panoramic view of her. I was so smitten by her beauty. I wish I could have told her all that I wanted to. Still, I thought I had done pretty okay. At least now I felt I was in the groove.

I saw Dev fluttering his hands ahead of me. The bastard had come. Never mind, nice try, I thought.

"Why are you carrying the bananas?" Nikita asked as Dev got into the car.

"Standard breakfast," he replied "milk and four bananas in the morning, good for my body." He said as he showed his biceps. *Damn him!*

"So Harsh, all okay," he winked at me from behind, I could see it in the mirror. I adjusted it to get a view of the traffic behind me.

"Yeah," I replied.

"So Nikita, why are you such a baby?" Dev asked as he devoured his bananas.

"What?" Nikita couldn't understand the question.

"Why do you need us to apply your passport, it's a pretty simple task."

"No it isn't, I can't stand those lazy bastards in a government office, I need someone for moral support."

"Moral support, huh," Dev said as he lowered the window pane to throw the peel of his fruit.

"Fuck! Why did you throw it out?" I asked.

"So what dude, this is India, there is garbage everywhere."

"That's because idiots like you dump it on the roads." Nikita replied.

"So what difference does it make if I don't throw, our country would anyway be an open garbage bin?" And he threw another one and then another.

"Yeah okay, you are not completely wrong." I said as I saw a huge heap of garbage dumped on the road towards my left.

Over the next ten minutes or so we spoke about how dirty our country was and how something should be done about it. All of us were however, cynical. We criticized about our politicians, our unethical people, inefficient law and police, corruption and 'I don't give a fuck' attitude.

One thing was definitely common in our conversation – we all hated being an Indian.

As we were approaching the passport office, I saw the traffic signal ahead about to turn red. I pressed the accelerator hard to avoid getting stuck in the two minute red light. I swerved my car, handling the steering deftly; Nikita would have sure been impressed by my maneuver. As I was about to cross, the light turned to an ominous red, but I continued at my speed, hell-bent to be on the other side of the road.

"Harsh easy baby," Nikita cried as she held out her long arms against the dash board.

Baby!! I liked it. For a second my mind got distracted by that word and that was enough reason together with my high speed to bang into a scooter that was crossing me from left to right.

"Oh shit!" I exclaimed more out of fear than of guilt as I saw people around us coming to help out the man and woman who fell from their god damn two wheeler. *Fucking idiots, didn't they see I was coming at such a speed?*

"We are screwed now Harsh, run if you can." Dev screamed from behind.

I thought as much. Bloody hell, accidents are an everyday affair of this country, so what if I caused one. But if I stay here, these guys would beat me to death. I looked at the other side at the couple whom I hit, they were doing pretty okay.

Fuck it, I thought. I pressed the accelerator and honked to move the crowd who had gathered infront of me. That was one of the reasons I hated India, everybody had all the fucking time to be a part of a commotion. I guess it was a source of entertainment for them. I didn't seem to care and drove past them with all my speed and within a minute I was clear of all the shit.

"Good Harsh, narrow escape." Dev hooted from behind.

"Fuck you guys, atleast you could have stopped and helped." Nikita said.

"It was nothing, don't worry," I replied, "they'll be okay, it was a minor accident."

"But I thought they were hurt, Harsh."

"Next time you see, they will be careful before coming infront of my car, ha." I breathed a sigh of relief now.

I looked at the front mirror to catch a glimpse behind. Far away I could still see the crowd; thank god no one was following us. I am sure I had left a traffic jam behind me.

Never mind, I continued cautiously for the remaining part of my journey. Within the next five minutes we reached our destination.

The passport office of Delhi is situated right behind the five star hotel 'Hyatt' amidst a horde of other complexes and offices. There is a car parking adjacent to them which is always packed owing to its trivial size compared to the people that visit the huge area on a daily basis. The cacophony of all sorts of sounds and polluted air was a characteristic of this place. I proceeded towards the car parking area and found a space for my car amidst the plethora of other cars.

"Oh that was a bad ride Harsh." Nikita punched me as we came out of the car.

I smiled.

"Twenty rupees." The weird looking parking man demanded the money from us. He checked out Nikita from the corner of his eyes. Bloody asshole, I felt like having another accident.

"It says ten rupees," I replied, pointing towards the yellow ticket slip he gave me.

"Yeah but we take twenty or take your car out from here." he said adamantly.

"Give it dude." Dev said.

"Here," I gave twenty bucks to that asshole, "why the hell do you have that attitude?"

"What?" he rebuked, giving me a baleful stare as he walked past us.

I sighed.

I don't know how I was planning to propose Nikita in the crowd bustling place as this. I had to find a way out somehow. Dev was ahead of me walking with Nikita. I wanted to tell her that lets get out of this place, forget the passport, and let's just live in India. But I knew it wasn't going to be as simple as that.

As we were approaching the office we were constantly pestered by touts who claimed to get us the passport in the earliest time possible. There were many of them standing not more than ten metres apart from each other. Nikita looked behind to ask me if we should get it done from them. I shook my head and signaled her to continue walking. The last thing I wanted was her passport to be ready in the next ten days. That would have been insane. Atleast with the normal process, it would take over a month, so that would give me enough time to convince her. But whatever said and done, I was really amazed at our Indian system. Just hundred meters away from the office, there were more than two dozen people who had the contacts to bribe our government officials so that the passport could be ready in less than ten days. However our lazy officials won't do it so early without the bribe. Man, I so love my country.

As we reached the office, we were beckoned towards the far end of the office which was behind, by some security staff who had red coloured teeth. They seemed very tired for eleven in the morning as they slouched on their chairs. When we reached, we were distressed to see the long queue infront of all the counters.

"Oh crap, now which line is ours?" Nikita asked.

"There," I pointed, "we have to take the form first." I was hoping for the forms to be over.

"I want to go to the loo man," Dev said, "this is going to take a while"

"Yeah, me too." I replied.

"But where are you going to find a washroom in this shitty place?" Nikita asked as we stood behind the long queue. I could tell that there were atleast thirty people infront of us. I don't know but the hard working man at the counter was taking more than two minutes for each person for a work which should take less than half a minute. That roughly translated into atleast an hour just for the form.

"Ha, ha, ha, Nikita this is India, you can pee just about anywhere here, that's the beauty of our country." Dev replied.

We high-fived! "We'll be back in ten minutes, okay, will have a smoke as well, don't move from here."

"You guys, peeing in the public huh, I hate it." But we were already gone.

We walked towards a small building that was adjoining the office. Few cars were parked infront of it. That seemed to be a perfect place for our little escapade.

"Come Dev, let us two bros make this land fertile, ha."
Dev obliged.

We did it. It is never more pleasant than pissing under the open sky.

"So when do you plan, huh?" Dev asked casually, zipping up his pants.

"Soon," I replied, "I don't know but this damn thing is taking a huge toll on me."

"Love dude," he said, "that's what it does, makes you forget everything else."

I don't know if Dev even understood what he said. We came to a small shop within the complex. We asked for a coke and a cigarette each. Guess I needed one to blow the tension within. I had serious doubts on how that helped though.

"Where the hell have you guys been?" Nikita shrieked when she saw us, "it's been fifteen minutes."

"Sorry," I said. I always love the sullen look on her face. It made her cheeks red, flushed with innocence. "The line looks pretty much the same."

"Fuck it is, you know only two guys have passed since then, this feels like an eternity."

"Relax Nikita," Dev said throwing his cigarette butt in the air.

In a way it was good, I sincerely hoped the line never ended and Nikita changed her mind. No passport meant no America. But I could see the growing impatience on her face as the 'sarkari babu' slowly moved his hands and indulged in gossip with his counterpart in the adjacent counter. They hated working, I could see that.

"Hey Nikita," I began, "come on let's go from here, it is crazy waiting this way, I'll find you a good and rich guy instead."

"What?" she beamed, "you can be funny Harsh."

"I know," I acknowledged with a wink in my eyes, "seriously Nikita, please don't leave us, we'll miss you."

"Who? You or Dev?"

"Me of course, I don't know about him though."

"And why would you miss me?" she asked coquettishly.

Why did she ask that? Was she flirting with me? What does she want to hear? Should I say it?

I was sure Dev had his ears fixed on our conversation. He kicked me from behind; perhaps even he felt this was the time. Okay, I thought, time had come.

"Nikita, that's because, I, umm, you know, I......."

Just then, the gentleman next to me in the adjacent line spat with brute force. "Aaathoooo."

The red coloured spit juxtaposed with paan fell on my shoes and jeans. For a moment I didn't believe what happened. My light blue coloured jeans had a huge red stain and drops of spit fell from it on my shoes.

"Oh crap, what the fuck is wrong with you?" I yelled at the *asshole*.

"Sory sory, mishtake bhaisahab," he slurped through a mouthful of paan.

How much space does he have in there?

"What sorry huh," Nikita screamed this time, "who's going to clean this shit." She pointed towards his saliva on me.

The *asshole* sheepishly took out his handkerchief from his pocket and gave it to her. She took it and meticulously tried cleaning the mess. I couldn't even look at it, forget cleaning. "Thanks Nikita," I said.

She continued her cleaning.

Other people in the queue also noticed my misery and had a sympathetic look in their eyes. Some of them were laughing. I wanted to tell them all to beat the asshole, but I guess there wasn't any point.

"What bhaisahab, you can't find any other place to spit." Dev spoke this time. He had a look of disgust on his face.

"Sory I wanted to spit away from him, mishtake sory."

"What away from him, are we standing in a dustbin, bloody asshole?" Nikita said looking up.

The *asshole* finally, dejected and embarrassed, turned his face away from us.

"Forget it Nikita, let it be, thanks for the cleaning, it's okay now."

She got up and threw the wet handkerchief on his face.

"Sory, mishtake bhaisahab," she said curtly.

"Nikita, really let's go from here," I said. More than my wet jeans, I was more disgusted at the *asshole* because finally I had mustered the strength somehow to say those three golden words and he screwed it up just like that. Had it not been for his spit, we might have been holding hands now. It was going to be a while now before I try doing it again.

"Wait Harsh, just five more people ahead now, we have already spent almost an hour standing like that."

"Okay," I looked at Dev. He signaled me to be patient.

I looked at my watch, it was already past noon. Just then, we were pushed by a strong jolt from behind by a group of 'civilized and ethical people'. They were not fond of standing in queues and waiting for their turn. They fought their way and came towards the counter. Everyone in the line abused and yelled at them. But they were brave people and gave two hoots of what others had to say or think about them. Nikita, as candid as she always is, was about to blast at them; but me and Dev stopped her observing their rowdy behaviour. However, Nikita couldn't control her urge.

"Hey you, can't you see the line, go stand behind and wait for your turn."

"Oye madam, we are the line, come stand behind us, ha, ha, ha," one of them barked while the other three sneered. The way they looked at her, irked me and Dev. We came forward and moved Nikita behind. *Game on mother fuckers!*

"Look now, the two brothers are here, ha, ha," they all laughed. Both of us just stared at them. Two minutes later, their work was done and they left but not without a lascivious glare at Nikita and a cold shoulder at me. This city or maybe this country can never be safe for women, I could see that.

"See Harsh, that's the reason I don't want to live in this stupid country, people spitting in the open, jumping queues, teasing women; I really want to be out of here."

I nodded submissively. *What else could have I done?* She wasn't wrong; we are a country full of these people. We ourselves weren't too good either, we throw garbage on our roads; I almost killed two people and then sped off from there. I was so used to these feelings that had a shade of guilt imbued in them. However, I forgot about it the next minute.

Our turn finally came. Nikita stooped to ask for a form.

"What form do you want?" the hard working man behind the counter screamed. Guess he was too tired.

"Passport application form."

"You still don't have a passport, how old are you?" I don't why but the guy was rude. Maybe it was the work load or maybe he was an asshole.

Nikita collected the form, gave him the money and didn't reply.

"What was with him?" she asked us as we came out of the queue.

"He's a government employee, he can afford to do or say whatever he wants to, who will stop him?" Dev condemned, "well atleast he gave you the form."

She filled the form in ten minutes, got the photocopies of her originals done from a nearby shop and we were back – in a queue, only this time in a separate one, the one where forms are submitted.

Like is always with Indian queues; people jump numbers, instead of a line we crowd at the window like a herd till we are ushered back to form a line again, but a minute later we all disintegrate and the 'rule of the jungle' applies – the mighty always wins. None of us made a fuss about it and waited for our turn. It did come finally after half an hour.

Nikita peeped through the small window and passed her papers. The guy on the other side appeared to be the enemy of humanity. He carried a forlorn expression and had the most depressing face I had ever seen. The oil slick hair and the slovenly moustache only added to his woes. He had a look at the papers and slammed them out of the window.

"How much have you studied?"

I completely failed to understand his uncouth behavior.

"I'm a graduate." Nikita replied sternly.

"You don't know how to sign then?"

"What?"

"Self attest all your papers and come again, get lost."
He threw the other papers as they fell on the floor. "Next,
quickly, quickly," he shouted.

"Fuck that is crazy, what kind of a behavior is that?"
Nikita was speechless and so were we. "Why do these
people have so much of an attitude? After all they are
made to sit over there for our service."

We felt so helpless, there wasn't any choice. Nikita
had to sign them and go back to the same window, the
same person and maybe get ill-treated again.

"Nikita its okay, that's how a government office works,
we have to take their shit." Dev said.

"But why?" Nikita asked, "I have filled my form,
submitted the papers and fees, that's the requirement
right? He is not doing any favour on me."

"Come on Nikita, just let it be, sign your papers, we'll
give it from here, no need to stand in the queue again," I
said.

Nikita shook her head in disbelief. "I'm out of here."

For a moment, I felt ecstatic. *Wow she's not applying
for it, so no more America.* My misconception was cleared
with her next statement.

"Let's go to those touts outside, its better I give them
extra money, atleast I don't have to go through this shit."

I looked at Dev, he smiled. Guess he had thought
likewise.

Nikita led us outside of the office and caught hold of
the first tout that came her way. She didn't even wait for
us and handed over her papers and discussed about the

time and money. A minute later she showed us the thumbs up sign. It was done.

"Congrats," I said as we walked towards her. She smiled back.

"So you bribed him, huh?"

"Fuck you Harsh, don't get started with that stupid Indian shit of yours again, that's the way it works here."

"Ha, ha, ha, never mind buddy," Dev tapped me from behind.

"Of course," I said.

8

SCREW IT! LET'S DO IT!

I had been failing miserably at the one thing I wanted to do so badly. My inability to express my feelings to Nikita had disappointed me to the hilt. I don't why I didn't have the courage to talk it out with her. I cried my heart out and couldn't resist my tears.

My mother had asked me a couple of times when I came back from the passport office three days back about the outcome of my proposal, but I always ignored her question. I felt like a loser. Maybe I was better off in my solitude. Nothing in my life had ever caused me so much pain, not even the divorce of my parents.

Why the hell did I fall in love?

Unlike everybody else, I hated being in love.

As the days passed, I felt as if the love of my life was gradually slipping from my hands. Soon a month would pass and then she would be gone, maybe forever. I had no hopes of anything happening after that. I had only about a month left. My heart beat increased at the thought of passing time. The clock ticked second by second.

What the hell am I doing? Why I am not stopping her? Hell, why I don't call her and tell her now?

As logic and sense dawned on me, I reached out for my phone that lay on the table. I thought about initiating the elusive talk. Though I had rehearsed it a multitude of times, I still wasn't sure how to go about it.

Screw it! Let's do it!

I searched the phone book to dial her number. My blood ran cold in my veins. But before I could dial her number, my phone rang.

It was her.

Oh my god, telepathy is it? There was definitely some connect there, I presumed. I accepted the call.

"You won't believe what just happened?" Nikita cried uproariously. Her excitement knew no bounds.

"What?" I asked. I was hoping something about us.

"I just got a mail from the ULCA university, they have accepted my application for the MBA, isn't that great?"

I was devastated. My hands began to tremble and tears found their way out from my eyes yet again. *Why was this happening to me?*

"Hey what happened? Are you there?"

"Yeah, it's great." I tried faking an elated voice.

"Isn't it?"

"So when would you be leaving?"

"Maybe next to next month, I just called the guy at the passport office, he said it wouldbe ready in another seven days maximum."

"Oh, so you set already," I gasped.

"Yes I am."

"Great, I'll talk to you later, bye."

I hung up, couldn't take it anymore, her happiness caused misery to me. I didn't even feel like a friend to her anymore. I guess it was pointless to do or say anything else. Nothing was going to stop her now.

Fine! I tried making peace with myself. I don't know why but I switched on my computer and logged on to facebook.com. I got a shock of my life when I saw 67 friend requests on my screen. *How many days had passed?* I pondered, ten maybe, at the most fifteen. It had worked that fast. I accepted them one by one. They were my old school friends, some batch mates from navy, few neighbours et al. Now I had 69 friends in all. It was amazing, guess now I should get used to living in the apparent world. I clicked on Nikita's profile and then her pictures. I ran my eyes through them one by one. I sighed. *So it was done then, she was going.*

I thought about communicating with her when she would be gone. Perhaps Dev was right, we should video chat. The lamest thing now appeared to be my solace. In the coming months that would be my only way to look at her pretty face.

I logged out and threw my computer before lying on my bed. I buried my face inside the pillow.

I think I did cry a little before sleep took over.

9

THE INCIDENT

W̶E had been summoned to Meerut - the second largest city in Uttar Pradesh. Our friend from school Ankit was getting married to his childhood love Gopika. Though it remains a mystery to me after atleast a dozen break ups, how on earth were they ending up with each other? Maybe it was love or perhaps destiny. I did believe in the latter after completely losing faith in the former. If something is meant to be, it will be; love had got nothing to do with it. Yes, I was a cynic. Love had made me one.

I was in no mood to drive for the three hours on the National Highway – 58 that connected Delhi to Meerut. I and Nikita drove to Dev's place who was our driver for the day. It amazed me when I saw Nikita's one day luggage. The blue coloured voluminous Adidas bag could have even accommodated her. It was full to the brim.

"What are you carrying in that huge bag?" I asked her, "the bride, is it?" Nikita laughed. My heart flinched. *What had her smile got to do with my damn heart?*

"I'm a girl Harsh; I'll be staying the night over. There is my sari to start with for the occasion, the makeup kit, accessories, few sandals to see which one matches best, another sari just in case the first one doesn't look good and then another set of........"

"Got it Nikita, thank you," I said. I had a look at my own bag pack; there was a little short for the night and some food for the journey.

Dev came out empty handed, "come let's go". He looked good in his blue coloured suit, only the tie wasn't matching.

"We've been waiting asshole," said Nikita. It was more than an hour we waited for the moron in his house.

Six in the evening was a really bad time to be on a Delhi road, thanks to the snail-paced traffic it offers its inhabitants. Add to it the maniacal driving sense of our people. Just outbound of Lajpat Nagar and we were stuck in what appeared to be a 'man-made traffic jam'. A car had hit another. The driver of the car hit had blocked the already bottle-neck road and was out to fight with the driver of the car who had hit. Both were oblivious to the mess they had created and abused each other's mothers and sisters. I guess people in this city or rather country need a reason to fight. Perhaps it was a panacea to our dull and monotonous life. One by one as the cars kept clearing, there was a flurry of abuses in the air. After about an hour or so we managed to be out, Dev hung his head out and performed the ritual of abusing the drivers of the two cars. They obliged by returning the favour.

"Get a life guys," Nikita screamed too, "move out you two."

I don't know what agreement they were coming on by not moving from there. I so loved my country.

We were quiet for the next fifteen minutes or so and reveled in the music on FM. Nikita sat behind and her makeup kit was already out. I had to get her off my mind so I thought of indulging in a conversation.

And what could be more fun than Dev's stupid girlfriends.

"So Dev, what about Neha? Where have you guys reached so far?"

Dev gave me a cold stare. "I hate her; I don't even want to talk about her."

I laughed. "What happened buddy, I thought you really liked her."

"Who's Neha now?" Nikita spurted from behind. She was running some sort of a machine through her hair, probably a hair straightener or something. What was the need, I thought, they looked so pretty anyway.

"His girlfriend from the gym," I replied.

"Not anymore," Dev spoke through a melancholic expression.

"Why, she got married is it?" I and Nikita broke into a guffaw of laughter.

"No," Dev replied.

"Thank god."

"She got engaged."

"What? No way, again?"

I don't know why we were being such asshole friends, but we laughed our stomachs out at his misery. Nikita stopped whatever she was doing with her hair.

"Yeah," he replied sheepishly, "she said I reminded of her ex boyfriend whom she claimed to be still in love with."

"What?" And the hysteria continued.

"Laugh you fuckers, you know that bitch actually thanked me, she said she owes her bloody re-union to me."

"Oh nice, she was so courteous."

Dev gave me a portentous stare.

"Ha, ha, stop it Dev you'll kill us with your jokes." Nikita said.

"This is not a joke you bitch, I don't know what is happening with my life, will I ever get married?"

"Marriage, huh?" I sighed.

"Dev please be away from me, atleast I don't want to be married now," Nikita said, "you got some serious hook up problem."

Oh so she doesn't even want to get married now, what the hell does she even want?

"Anyway Dev, all the best with your next one." I said.

Few more discussions and a lot more traffic jams and we reached our destination. A three hour journey was completed in five hours, but the good part – we reached safe and sound. We were led into the driveway of the hotel by the staff and Dev handed over his car for the valet. From the very onset, the gala appeared to be huge and pompous, what one could expect of a Punjabi wedding. The hotel 'Naveen' was draped with flashing lights and flowers all along its periphery. People around were dressed ostentatiously, women had jewellery all over their body. Guess they waited for these days to showcase whatever they had!

We met Ankit's big brother who was dressed in a blazing white sherwani. He guided us to the rooms where we could change and get ready for the occasion. I and Dev looked at each other and smiled, *do we look like we need to change?* Needless to say, Nikita rushed towards the room, I followed her carrying her luggage. I was thrown out of the room as soon as we entered and Nikita asked for an hour to be ready. When I came out, Dev was already gorging on the snacks and drinks.

"Hey, stop eating, did you meet Ankit?"

"No, not yet," he replied through a mouthful of chicken tikka.

"Come let's go then."

We entered the little room on the alleyway towards the left which was reserved for the very special guests by Gopika's parents. It was flocked by the entire family of the groom. We brushed past them to finally catch a glimpse of Ankit who already looked tired. He also wore a blazing white sherwani; a closer look revealed it was exactly the same as his brother's.

"You fuckers couldn't find different clothes?"

"Hey there you guys, so finally you came, huh," Ankit replied ignoring Dev's question.

"Fuck you Ankit, you haven't even shaved properly, it's your marriage today."

"Really," he asked me as he ran his hands over his face. There was atleast a dozen of hair strands protruding through his face. "Oh shit, Gopika is going to kill me." He ran outside, perhaps towards his room. I smiled, why are guys so scared of girls?

It was already nine and we were damn hungry. We proceeded towards the snacks' counter and were amazed by the variety of snacks offered. Anyone having an opinion on India's poverty should first definitely attend a Punjabi wedding; there was so much food here, enough to feed an entire village of our country. And we had not even seen the main course yet. Whoever said India is poor?

Shunning the patriotic thoughts, we ate and drank as much as we could. In between Dev did try to strike a conversation about Nikita but I ignored him. There wasn't any point talking about it, I said. If it was meant to be, destiny would conjure it for me anyway.

We continued eating and drinking. Dev ushered me outside for a smoke. The free alcohol had already started showing its effects. There were a few rowdy men from the party in a state of drunken stupor. They were shouting and screaming on the roads and abusing to everyone that passed by. Perhaps, it was their idea of having fun. They even stopped cars that went by just like that and abused them.

"What's with those idiots, dude?" Dev asked me. I don't know why he was expecting I had an answer to that.

"They are Indians, what else." I replied, I guess that pretty much was the answer. I don't know why we Indians are so proud of our culture and history when one of the highest rape cases and harassment against women are filed here. People die of hunger and unemployment while corruption is at its peak. The excess food rots because there isn't enough storage space and the government sleeps over it. And then we have got such maniacs in our country. I guess we people are hypocrites of the highest order.

"Hey what are you thinking now, Nikita is it? Come let's go back in," Dev offered.

"Right," I said following him.

Inside, the bride had finally arrived. People gathered around her to have a cursory look. I have known Gopika since our school days and I know she'd make a pretty bride. There were whispers around the hall and I could say it had to be about her, probably comparisons with

Ankit, about her lehenga, her attitude and gait. *Why can't people mind their own business?*

And then came Nikita; I hadn't seen a prettier thing than that in my entire life. She appeared as if she came straight from heaven. Her eyes, gleamed with vivacity, and were outlined by the blue liner which matched immaculately with her lehenga. Her hair had light curls that gradually culminated towards the end. *Wasn't she straightening them in the car?* As she was walking, her eyes darted everywhere, probably to locate us. Dev signaled towards her. Every moment as she walked towards us, I had this immense feeling of anxiety that over powered me. I had this urge of kissing her at that very moment, but acquiesced a second later that I had to wait for it now or maybe my entire life.

"Isn't she looking beautiful," Nikita asked, looking at Gopika.

"Yes, beautiful." I replied looking at Nikita.

After the befitting jaimal ceremony, where the bride and groom put garlands around each other's necks, we were greeted by the not so melodious sound of the drums. They had pretty much the same rhythm for hours. People poured around them and danced wildly with exaggerated emotions. Nikita too was a part of it and took Dev for company; she knew I couldn't dance so Dev had to be her choice. Owing to the small area of the hall, the entire troop found their way outside on the roads. At eleven in the evening, traffic wasn't much of a concern in a city like this. However the huge uproar would definitely be not welcomed by the neighbouring houses.

And it wasn't.

Few minutes later, residents of the nearby houses came down and requested to atleast stop the clamour of drums. They were not completely wrong, I thought, what had they done wrong to be punished like this? But few uncles of Ankit didn't think likewise. In an alcoholic haze they abused and yelled at them.

"Oye, behenchod it's our son's wedding, we will celebrate it, do whatever you have to."

And so it began, the game we Indians are best at – fighting at menial issues. No wonder the Britishers deployed the divide and rule policy on us. It was not an intelligent idea as many had thought it was; any dumb prick could have thought about it after living for some time with us. We Indians just have to fight. That's the way this country runs.

In a minute the atmosphere of celebration evaporated and the air was filled with enmity. There were kicks and abuses and everyone joined the party. Alcohol helped the cause. Soon Ankit and Gopika's parents came rushing out to intervene in the unwonted spat. People were requested to behave and the loud music was stopped. Ankit's uncles did concede but not without their last minute acridity.

"Behenchod sale, what they think of themselves, they don't know who we are?" The statement was neither a question nor an answer and no one bothered replying. The crowd disappeared and soon everything was forgotten. Food stalls were opened and everybody was attracted to their pleasant whiff. It's amazing how good food can make you forget anything, atleast for the time being. The three of us also picked up our plates and proceeded to the counter. The menu was gargantuan and had almost every Indian dish that existed. And then there were Chinese, Italian and Mexican counters too. More than half of the food was definitely getting wasted here. What a shame, when more than half our country was living below the poverty line, so much of food was being wasted. I made a pact with myself that day, to get married in a court and not throw such a lavish party for morons to drink and forget about it. That was ofcourse if I was getting married in the first place, if not Nikita it will take a long time to get over her and find a new girl.

It was already past midnight and we decided to leave. We had atleast a three hour drive towards Delhi and that wasn't a very safe thought. Delhi can be really dangerous at night owing to the truck drivers who rule the roads. We bade our goodbyes to the bride and groom who were busy amidst the plethora of guests and photo shoots. It was mandatory for them to have a picture clicked with everyone in the room with a full wide smile. I did pity them.

Outside Dev's car arrived and he tipped the waiter with a ten rupee note. Quite generous of him, I thought for a miser like him. We had a couple of drinks each and that made me ponder if we were in a state to drive.

"Nikita, would you mind driving?" I asked her, her eyes were barely open.

"Why can't Dev drive?"

"Because he's drunk and so am I."

"Oh shut up Harsh, four drinks won't do any harm, I'll drive."

"Hey but that's illegal, you can't drink and drive, what if the cops catch us."

"The cops, ha, ha, this is India dude, all your so called cops would have slept themselves after a hard day's work and a bottle of liquor."

"Yeah, but...."

"Don't worry man, we'll throw Gandhiji on their faces and they'll wag their tail like a dog." He said flipping the five hundred note at me. Either he was too drunk or the note was fake, he doesn't have that big a heart to bribe so much.

"Okay," I conceded, the car was his, he was driving, the fake note belonged to him, then what the heck?

Just when Dev got on the driver's seat, something crossed Nikita's mind and she offered to drive. "Dev let it be, I guess Harsh is right, you are too drunk to drive. It's got really strict these days."

"Okay," Dev conceded.

After twenty minutes of silence, Dev asked for a cigarette from behind.

"It's over." I replied.

"Yeah I had the last one." Nikita said.

"Oh I want one now," Dev cried. It's hard to understand the relation between a cigarette and alcohol; both are incomplete without each other.

After five minutes we saw a small gloomy little shop on the edge of the road. It had a low power bulb arched on top to indicate its presence on the dreary road.

"Hey, there I guess you might find your fag."

Nikita swerved the car towards the right and stopped inches before the shop. Glad, she didn't bang it. No wonder men stay away from female drivers on roads.

We took three cigarettes and lit them.

"Hey Harsh, come let's make this land fertile, I really want to pee."

"Okay, brother, let's do it."

Suddenly we heard someone ranting from behind. At first we didn't pay any attention. As awareness dawned on us, we realized it was for us.

"Oye bastards what are you doing here so late in the night?"

We squinted in the dark to see. A tall frame with broad shoulders stared back at us. He wore a khaki coloured uniform in a rather slovenly fashion.

"Brajesh sahib, here your cigarettes," the shop keeper offered in panic.

"Nothing, just….." I tried replying with a shrug of my shoulder but was interrupted by him.

"I know you motherfuckers, drinking at night and creating trouble."

"Hello," Nikita said, "we are not creating any trouble, look at you, you are a police officer and drinking on duty, I'll complain that."

Without further ado, the cop slapped her so hard she fell on the floor, "bitch you'll complain about me, a cop?"

"Sir, how dare you slap her, what wrong have we done?" Dev said.

"I'll tell you what wrong you have done," he caught hold of Dev's neck, "you bastards have the balls to question police, Mahesh, come here, take them to thaana, I'll show them what I can do."

And just like that, two constables emerged from behind, handcuffed us three, kicked and abused us till their jeep.

"Today I'll show you behenchods what I can do."

He threw the bottle of rum on the road in a fitful rage and started the engine.

10

THE ANNA HAZARE CAMPAIGN

Three weeks later....

WE were still in a state of shock and not over the gruesome incident on the night of our friend's wedding. I couldn't believe it happened to us. We had seen similar incidents on TV, read about them in news papers and magazines, but it always felt like a delusion. India is not that unsafe a country, I had always thought. But that day changed it all. I shuddered over the images that still loomed in my mind. I wondered what Nikita would be going through.

We had just met once since that day and couldn't even look in each other's damp eyes. We were still scared and ill at ease when we spoke. I know things could have never been the same again. Two days back when me and Dev had gone over to Nikita's place, she hid in her bedroom and refused to meet anyone. Somehow, we managed to sneak into her room. My heart cried at her sight. She appeared dull and gloomy. We sat next to her.

"Hey, you alright Nikita?" I asked.

She was quiet. I knew it wasn't an appropriate question. "Didn't I tell you Harsh, I hate India and never want to be here." She finally spoke; her hollow voice trembled through her mouth. And then she started crying. I hugged her and looked at Dev. He was crying too. I had no clue how to react or what to say. I was myself tormented. But I knew time would heal our wounds, as it always does. I guess it was better to leave her alone for few more days to recuperate.

When I reached my home, I couldn't do anything. There was something bothering me incessantly and it did before the incident as well. That day only aggravated it. I couldn't sleep or eat; I couldn't even concentrate on anything. Time and again I thought if our country was really that bad or was it our people? Was Nikita right? Should we all leave this stupid country? I don't know from where but a guilt factor had crept in. Somehow I also felt a bit responsible for all the mess in the country. I don't think I had been a good citizen and neither do Dev and Nikita. *Do we really have a right to complain?*

I know there wasn't any point discussing a futile thing as this, whatever had to happen has happened and I know we'll never forget it for the rest of our life. Time would sure heal the wounds, but the scars would always remain.

I switched on the TV to divert my mind from these thoughts. And there, he was back. Anna Hazare had again threatened the government to produce a suitable Lokpal Bill which suited the nation's interest, else he would go on another fast unto death campaign from August 16, 2011. I revered the courage of the man, his determination and self-less attitude. I wish I could be like him. He did not grumble, did not complain about the system, just believed in the power of action. The entire nation supported him and the news channels were behind him. For once atleast a man stood up to fight against the corrupt. I definitely thought of supporting him and decided to be at Jantar Mantar in Delhi where he was voicing his campaign. That was the least I could have done to pacify my inner calling. I knew I could manage to convince Dev to come along; Nikita would have been out of question.

However on the morning of 16th August, Anna Hazare along with his aides was remanded to judicial custody for seven days as the entire nation watched in horror. The police action, it was believed, was taken at the behest of some cabinet ministers. This arrest set off protests across the entire country which spread like wild fire. Grueling under pressure, the Delhi police said they were ready to release him on a personal bond provided he assures them that he would not defy section 144 of the Criminal Procedure Code which prohibits the gathering of five or more people.

Much to the dismay of Anna's supporters and the entire country, he was taken to the Tihar jail in Delhi under judicial custody along with other leading activists. Anna said that this was the beginning of the "second freedom struggle". He refused food and water in jail, indicating that he would carry on with his fast even in Tihar jail.

After protests all over India, the Delhi police finally conceded to release Anna, however, he refused to leave the jail until the government agreed to give him unconditional permission to hold protests unlike last time. Finally, he got permission to fast for 15 days at Ramlila Maidan.

Anna Hazare finally left Tihar jail on 19th August after spending 3 days in custody. His release bought a wave of relief to the entire country and he was welcomed by his supporters.

19th August, I and Dev were outside the Tihar jail along with a horde of other supporters. There was a huge gathering outside the jail to welcome Anna Hazare and he was greeted with a huge roar when he came out and shouted "Bharat mata ki jai". He also said "whether I'm here or not this fight will continue". There was a huge round of applause. Anna then waved the Indian flag at us. All of us responded by waving smaller flags and enchanting "Long live Anna".

Finally he reached Ramlila Maidan to launch his 15 day mass protest against corruption. He gave a little speech about how corrupt the system was and everyone associated with it and how each and every Indian should unite to see a better India. He was urging the government to draft the bill enacted by their civil society as theirs was not to be trusted.

I came back all enthused and motivated.

"If he can do this at such an age, why can't we Dev." I asked him in the car on our way back.

"Do what?" Dev appeared perplexed.

"Do our part," I replied.

"Come on Harsh, get a hold on to yourself, nothing is going to happen, our country sucks and will always do, how can you forget what happened to us, what wrong had we done, tell me?"

"I know that, but I'm fed up of blaming everybody around us but ourselves, I mean what have we done as citizens of this country? I know what happened was terribly wrong, we did not deserve that, atleast not Nikita but that can't be our excuse not to do anything and just sit and blame the system."

"I don't know man, this sounds weird to me, even if we do something what good can it bring, I mean there are 1.2 billion people in this country, nobody cares."

"I know nobody cares, but someday they would, and even if it doesn't make a huge difference, it's okay, atleast we should try, so that we can answer ourselves. Atleast then we'll have the right to complain about our country."

"Okay, fine, even if we decide doing something, what exactly can we do Harsh?"

"Frankly even I haven't thought about it, to start with, atleast change ourselves first. Look at us, we always complain about the dirt in the country but do we ever realize we also are behind this mess, we throw garbage on the roads, urinate in public and then blame the country; we don't follow traffic rules, drink and drive, that day I hit somebody and ran and then we blame the country for accidents; we bribe people to get the passport early, you cheat your customers, hell we don't even cast our votes but still we complain about everything around us. Don't you think this is unethical, okay I'm not saying this will make a significant difference but that is the least we can do."

"Look dude, we can do this but that won't change this country, or the mentality of our people, there is a huge population in here."

"I know that, but let's just do what we can, stop worrying about others, come on not all your customers buy your bullshit and eventually your car, but that does not stop you from lying to them, isn't it?"

"Oh that is different, you see."

"How is that different Dev, you don't care about the results but still do it because you have to, we do so many things in our life without caring for the results then why not this? Things would only change in this country when educated people like us act, but someone has to start, why can't that be us? Let's stop caring about what others have to do and how will it help, let's just do something."

"You are being over enthusiastic man really, but okay, I agree we are assholes too."

"Good, thanks."

"You know for starters we should set that bastard Brajesh straight, I mean how can he get
away from what he did that night?"

I sighed, I also wanted to do something about him, "you know we can't do anything now, he has the backing of the entire police with him, let the right time come, I swear I won't spare him."

I thought about that day, it still sent tremors down my spine. True it had shown what the powerful could do in this country and how unsafe India can be if you are nobody. I don't know why but this time I didn't feel like complaining, but actually doing something about it. It's easy to fret over the system and then forget about it, but this time I actually wanted to fight, do whatever I can in my own way. I know there wasn't a huge scope but atleast a full hearted try was all I wanted to give.

I thought about talking it out with Nikita too, but I knew it wasn't going to be easy after what she had been through. But atleast it would be better than crying and grouch over something that had already passed. The next day we went over to Nikita's house. Like expected she didn't want to meet us, that had to stop, she can't be doing that to herself.

"Nikita really sorry for that day, are you okay?" I hugged her as I entered the room.

"Yeah," she said in a gloomy voice, "how about you guys?"

"We have decided to do something about it."

"About what?"

"About what happened that day Nikita, about our mentality and attitude. We can't just keep quiet and sulk about what happened, something has to be done."

"I don't know what you are talking about Harsh, really?"

"So you are moving out of India?"

"Ofcourse, I am, I hate this country and always will, bastards like that police officer rule this country. I have to get out of this shit." She screamed at the top of her voice.

"Nikita I don't know what makes you think that this happens only in India, have you guys never heard of corruption outside this country, you think your America is not corrupt or any other developed nation for that matter. There is corruption in almost every country, it's just that their citizens are not too pessimistic as us, they have some belief in their government and leaders."

"Well I don't and can never will, bye Harsh see you guys later."

With that she switched off the lights. Dev ushered me to leave. He didn't look interested anyway; he was here only because I wanted him to. Never mind I was not going to give up so easily. I had made my mind; I had to do my part. And I never thought of doing something substantial, I knew it was the small things that make all the difference. The start was always important, the toughest part about any activity; after that things just fall in place on their own.

In some little corner of my mind, there was another thought. If I can do something worthwhile it might just entice Nikita to stay back. I knew this was my last shot but I had to do this.

I still loved her.

11

THE GROUP – 'THE INDIA
I DREAM OF'

I came back home with a flurry of thoughts. I had
no clue what I was going to do. There was only
a positive attitude and a will to do something good. Over
the next few days I wondered what I could do within my
scope. Clouds of doubt hovered over me as I had no clue
from where to start.

Few days passed and I was still wondering. I switched
on my TV and changed to a news channel. I needed some
serious motivation and what could be better than watching
Anna Hazare's speech.

There was another issue which he pressed. He wanted
the Prime Minister and the Chief Justice of India to be
also under the purview of the bill. The opposition parties
were in complete favour of that. I'm not sure if they even
cared about it, it was their chance to put the ruling party
down. There was a lot of agitation about the same and our
cabinet ministers were not in favour of the same. Their
point was that if the top echelons of the country cannot be

trusted then how can the country run? It will make people completely lose faith in the system.

Frankly even I was not much in favour of it. I didn't doubt the credibility of the man but somewhere I thought, he wasn't fasting for the right cause. The idea of a Lokpal bill which is basically an anti-corruption ombudsman is based on a Scandinavian model. I remember reading somewhere it was first enacted in the 1960s and didn't work then. There was not much of a chance that it would work fifty years later. Besides the creation of Lok Ayukta at the state level has not reduced corruption in the state governments, so I had serious doubts if its counterpart would be of much help at the national level.

Even if the draft of the bill presented by the civil society was accepted by the government and all his other demands, I'm not sure if that would really help. What was the guarantee that members of the Lokpal would not turn corrupt someday? And who would be watching them? There can't be another Lokpal to keep an eye on them. Besides what good will it do to the common man? This all sounded good but I did feel that nothing was happening at ground level. The poverty and illiteracy would still remain and somehow corruption would still breathe.

Over the next few days I pondered over my options. I didn't have many. There wasn't any point talking to Dev and Nikita as they weren't interested. All I wanted was to spread some awareness among as many people as I could that it is our country, do your part and be optimistic. Don't bother about the results and one day atleast our kids would see a better India. But as simple as that sounds I didn't even know where to start.

Just then I thought of facebook. I switched on my computer and logged on to the website. I had 55 more friend requests, guess it was because they were my mutual friends with the older ones. I accepted them all. I had more than 120 friends now. It was unbelievable. I thought of telling each one of them about my views but then rejected it the next moment. I saw options on the left hand side of the page to create a group or a page. I clicked on the 'create a group' icon. It asked for a name. I thought for a few minutes and typed: 'The India I dream of.' There could be three types of groups – open, closed or secret. I made it an open group so that anyone could see it. In the about section, I wrote the following:

"Time has come to stand united, to stop waiting but to act to see a better India. Remember the dialogue from the movie 'Rang De Basanti' that no country is perfect, it has to be made one; well time has come to make India a perfect country. There is nothing huge that we can do but lets atleast get started, make small differences and ignite the passion. Let's not care about the results, rather do something passionately for the country. Let's stop complaining and criticizing as always but act. Let's just shun away the thought that 'nothing's going to happen, nothing will change, this country would always suck'. Atleast once let's try and be positive! Remember as was famously quoted in the movie – this country will change, we'll bring about the change. "

With that I sent an invite to all my facebook friends and shared its link on my page. I know it didn't make any sense but hoped someone had a better idea. I requested all my friends to share the page with as many people as they could. It was lame, I know, people would laugh at me. But I had to do this. Sometimes just to satisfy your inner calling, people do stupid stuff, but as long as it makes you happy and content, what the heck?

I thought of calling off the day and planning for my little endeavour the following day. I logged out and shut my computer. The thoughts didn't leave my mind.

I wasn't going to give up.

12

THE LIST…

HOLY crap! What the hell happened? I was staring at my computer screen in bewilderment. This can't be happening. I had just woken up a few minutes ago and was having my morning dose of caffeine. Then it occurred to me to log on to facebook and just have a look at the group I created yesterday. And there it was – it had 363 members and 88 comments already. I looked at the watch. How much time had transpired? 10 hours, 12 hours at the most! And that too during the night! Don't people sleep? I couldn't believe what happened. To be frank I did expect a few likes and one odd comments, but that much? I was excited and fascinated at the same time. So what does that mean – there are actually so many people out there who feel likewise. I did believe that, I guess Anna Hazare had ignited the passion. Even if the Lokpal Bill does not end up the way he and every Indian in this country wants, he had atleast changed the people's perception. For once people actually started believing that some positive would come up and this country would change. I guess this was a good time for what I had planned. Edified, I started reading the comments. Some of them were from people I didn't even know, perhaps my friend's friends.

"Sure buddy, really appreciate that initiative. I guess if something has to change in this country we all have to get together. Would look forward to more from you!"

That was Tajinder Arora. I opened her profile, she was from Chandigarh. I had never even been there. Wow! I marveled at facebook. What a nice way to get your point across.

"Glad someone thinks the way I do, I am with you and so are my friends." Karan Bali from Pune.

"Wonderful thought! We are with you."

"Thanks, you are right, let's just for once do something and stand united."

"Okay buddy, from now on no complaining and criticizing my country."

"I agree."

But this is India, there had to be some negative and skeptical thoughts as well.

"I loved Rang De Basanti, but is it really possible?"

"Hey dude, I guess you are being too enthusiastic, it's not easy."

"This is India, it will never change, we people suck and will always do."

"All the best man, nice dream, ha!"

"I don't know what do you plan to do?"

Whoever that guy was, he wasn't totally wrong. I had absolutely no clue what I wanted to do. It was more like having fun on facebook. Nevertheless that did not deter my determination to atleast try. I kept reading the other comments, some of them inspired me and some made me feel like a donkey. But the overall effect had been quite overwhelming. It did enthuse me to carry on. I thought of sharing this with Dev. I called him.

"Hey there, you up?"

"Yeah, tell me, how come so early?"

"I have sent you an invite of the group I created yesterday. It's about that thing I was discussing with you the other day"

"Whatthing?"

"About India, dude."

"Oh crap, you are not over that shit yet, what the hell did you do now?"

"I have made a group on facebook and shared it; you know it's got famous overnight."

"Big deal Harsh, that's not because of your stupid idea; that is social networking for you."

"Yeah whatever, but atleast have a look."

"Okay, I will, you are being a complete idiot man, I don't know what are you thinking, why are you trying to become Mahatma Gandhi?"

"Shut up Dev, I'm serious about this."

"Serious about what, what is happening to you, nobody has the time for all this, people are so busy with their own life."

"Okay fine, let me just try what I have to."

"Okay buddy, do whatever, now can I please go, I have to get to work."

"Bye," I hung up. *Bastard!*

It wasn't a good idea calling him. Whatever little motivation I had got, evaporated! But was he right? Any other day I would have thought likewise, but I don't know from where I had got so much energy and will power.

Maybe it was the incident that day or maybe my last attempt to stop Nikita. Whatever it was, I was not going to give up.

I thought of taking it to the next level, maybe involving more people. But before that I had to think about something which would get us closer. I ruminated for a little while. I was looking for a common thread that binds us Indians. We were not very different from each other. We all hated our country and complained about it, but still somewhere a bit of a guilt factor lingered. We all wished doing something, but never knew what. I guess this was the time to make things clear for myself and others. I had facebook for a platform to share my thoughts with so many people out there.

It had to be something about us to start with. Charity always begins at home, as the age old adage goes. There are a multitude of things which we Indians do at a daily and regular basis which contributes to all the filth, anger and corruption in our country. That has to be sorted out first before we think about other things. I channeled my thoughts in that direction. I took out a piece of paper and started writing all that I hated doing at some point or the other in my life.

"Harsh, come breakfast is ready," my mother hollered from the kitchen.

"Later, I'm not hungry," I said and continued the little task. It wasn't taking much time once the thought was clear. Ten minutes later, I had a list of 5 things that I regret doing and swore that I would never do that again. I'm sure a lot of people would agree with me.

Then I posted it on the group page:

"Hello guys,

Glad to see all your comments, thanks. Let's just all get together and do something. I know it won't be easy and also it will be a lot of time when we actually start seeing results. Maybe it is stupid and would get us nowhere, but let's do something guys. After all it's our country; we can't keep quiet and sulk over it. **For starters we have to improve; each individual has to change - our mindset and our actions.** If we can do that only then we can expect others around us to change. Here's a list of few things that we shouldn't be doing. If you agree and swear by it, hit the 'like' button. Any worthwhile comments would be welcome.

1. We complain about our ministers, about our government, but frankly how many of us even bother casting a vote. Atleast I don't, and I can bet not many of you either. Then what could we be possibly complaining about? You think we have a right to grumble? I don't think so. We have to get rid of the thought that one vote wouldn't make any difference, the entire country is corrupt. First let's do our duty and only then expect others to do theirs.

2. It's a very common discussion that our country is dirty and full of filth, well does any of us realize we are equally responsible for that. We litter in open, urinate in public places, hardly use dustbins, spit but still have the audacity to complain. I shamefully admit that I do it all the time. If everyone stops doing it, we *will* see a difference, not immediately but sometime in our near future. Better late than never!

3. All of us complain about the accidents on Indian roads, the traffic jams and our inept driving sense. But how many of us realize we are the reason behind all

the mess. We over speed, run traffic lights, drink and drive, disobey traffic rules and well, cause accidents. I do it all the time but swear won't do it from today onwards. What about you guys?

4. Is India really corrupt or have we made it one. How many of you have bribed a government official? I'm sure every Indian at some point in his/her life has done it to get things done faster. Pay special attention to 'faster'. If it was not for the bribe, the work would have got done anyway but in its normal process taking the allotted time. But we guys are always in a hurry, I don't know why? Let's stop doing it, well atleast for this reason. We'll figure out what to do for other reasons in time.

5. Last but not the least, stop complaining. If you are so used to doing it, then first atleast do your part, change yourself. Be the perfect citizen and please get rid of the thought that what would happen if I change, there are a billion people out there. Be optimistic and do your part religiously and I can assure you a day would come when we'll see a change. India *would* become perfect!

Share this page and thought with as many people as you can if you want to see better results. Inspire people around you to incorporate the above in their life. Also I could think of just five points, lets increase that list, I'm sure there are a lot of other things that we Indians are doing wrong. Share your thoughts and we'll all follow it.

Keep watching out for this space.

Later,

Harsh

P.S. – Be the change you want to see in the world."

I read it aloud to myself. I guess it had come out pretty okay; it might just inspire few people. Not bad, I thought for a start. I got off from my bed and sauntered towards the kitchen.

I was damn hungry!

13

THANK YOU MARK ZUCKERBERG!

THE day went pretty much the same as always – boring. I had stopped calling Nikita and she didn't bother calling me too. I guess it was better off that way. We would remind her of that day all the time. Besides she might just be leaving in a few weeks' time for her coveted MBA that might just help her to move on and forget about it. That incident had taken a huge toll on her. It would have, on any other girl. I and Dev cursed ourselves for not being able to help her, but we were equally jeopardized. We never spoke about it till date, but I had seen it in his eyes when we last met. He would have seen it in mine too. I don't know what to call it – guilt, remorse, regret. It was not that we blamed each other for it, but just hoped we had more guts.

I could never get rid of those ghastly images in my head. I wish mind had a recycle bin too, past thoughts could be deleted, or if need be, restored in a click. I guess what I was doing now was a panacea to those ill-fated memories. An attempt to restore what we lost that day or perhaps to ensure it doesn't happen to anyone else.

We had not met each other for days now. Sundays also passed, the day when we *had* to be with each other. Dev and I spoke on the phone but only for a little while. I guess it would take some more time for things to be normal between us. Till then I had an important task ahead of me.

Late evening, I logged on to facebook again. I knew I was expecting way too much that early, it had been less than ten hours since my last post.

I was *so* wrong.

There were 225 likes and 167 comments already on my post. Apart from that, the group itself had over 800 members; that meant I could communicate with that many people with a single post of mine. Wow! Mark Zuckerberg we love you. A big thank you from India!

I went through all the comments one by one. People actually liked it and agreed to it. I was overjoyed.

"Done dude, count me in."

"Sure, that's the best way to start." That was Tajinder Arora, my first visitor on the page.

"Sounds good, Will do and ensure all others in my knowledge too."

"That makes sense, Harsh. Really appreciate your initiative, good going."

There were suggestions to increase the list as well. One of them read:

"Why can't we Indians ever follow queues, why can't we wait for our turn, why are we always in a hurry? Harsh please make this the sixth point in your list. We Indians have to learn to wait and be patient. Btw you are doing a great job!

Regards,

Puja from Mumbai"

Another read: "In relation to the traffic chaos, I like to add that I'm always struck with revulsion, why the hell do people always obstruct a free left or right and cause traffic jam behind? How much would they gain if they wait in their respective lane? A minute, 2 minutes perhaps! I don't know about other cities but in the metros, it happens all the time. When would we learn?"

Point noted Anuj; maybe I could include that in my list as well.

I read all the other comments; what was most pleasing was that there wasn't a single negative comment. Everyone had a positive outlook. I guess that's the advantage of keeping things simple. I just wondered if all the 800 members agree to my little plan in 2 days, how many would in a year? It felt great. My little endeavour had been successful so far.

So far so good!

"That's tremendous guys, thanks a lot for your inputs, but remember we have to abide by our rules, this won't go anywhere unless each one of us changes our self. Please share the link of this page on your profile so that more people can be aware of our little mission. Suggestions welcome!"

I read it once and then pressed enter. That was the 168th comment. I don't know where this was going, but it definitely was fabulous for a start.

I included the two suggestions which made my list to 7 points now. I hoped for more. I scratched my head to think if I had any, but it was in vain. I didn't seem to care much about it; enough work had been done already in the past two days. I wanted to tell Nikita about it, but I knew she would give a damn about it. Whatever little love she had for the country, vanished that day.

I waited for the right moment.

14

THE BLOG – "THE INDIA I DREAM OF"

I did not log on to facebook since the last two days, on purpose. Maybe I wanted to be struck with a surprise with a lot more people and comments or maybe I was scared. So far, it had been too good to be true. Within two days I had more than eight hundred people talking about it. How long would this continue? Maybe it was the initial spark which would eventually fizzle in a few days.

I was wrong yet again!

The sight of my computer screen filled me with awe. I was completely shocked. The members of my group had risen to more than three thousand now. My post about the list had more than 800 likes and over 300 comments. *What the hell was happening?* People were sharing the links of the group page on their profile and inviting their friends to join it. According to facebook statistics, on an average a person has 130 friends in his list. So assuming if even half of them saw the group it would still mean 500 times 65 which meant 3250 views already. And if that many people were to post it on their profile, that number multiplied by 65 again. And again and again and again! This was spreading like a wild fire.

I prided myself after reading the comments. There was appreciation and optimism throughout. People actually supported me and stood by my belief. Almost all of them said they would do their part and follow the list religiously, and that everybody they knew would do the same. There was no shade of negativity any more, people actually believed in it and wanted to do something, howsoever small it might seem. I wrote a usual thanks post and motivated people to continue sharing and changing yourself. I could see this was working, and the best part – the number of people rose exponentially each day. It was like magic.

But I got greedy; I wanted things to happen even faster. I thought of other ways of promoting the group page and spreading awareness. I know people liked the idea, it's just that more and more people had to know about it. That got me thinking. Greed is good, which is why I resorted to blogging. I guess that is another way to share your thoughts and ideas on the internet. Perhaps my inability to express my feelings to Nikita was another reason I took to writing. I didn't have to bother much about the name of my blog. It had to be 'The India I dream of'. I went to blogger.com, one of the websites that allows people to express their opinions for free on the internet. I fed in all the information and within minutes my account was ready. I thought about my first blog, the idea was pretty clear; I just scouted for the right words. Well honestly it was inspired by Anna Hazare and Baba Ramdev's recent campaign.

After completing the little speech about my country I posted it; my first blog. Hell, few months earlier I didn't even use the internet, I always considered it to be a waste of time. It wasn't, if used for the right reasons.

I posted the link of my blog on my facebook profile and the group I created few days back.

"For more insightful thoughts about our country, you might want to read my blog as well.

Feel free to post your comments."

And I added the link of my blog to our group page.

It felt good, I was trying to carve my niche as a writer, an inspirational one perhaps, someone who guides his readers into the right things. I had just one lesson for them – respect your country, do your part and be patient!

On that note I felt an urge to call Nikita. I did succeed in resisting it for nearly 45 seconds. Her phone rang, my heart beat rose.

"Hello," she finally answered in a morose voice, after eight rings. I don't know how much my pulse had shot upto for waiting so long.

"Hey Nikita, how have you been?"

"I'm okay."

"I have really missed you Nikita, you want a grab a cup of coffee sometime?"

"I'm not in the mood really Harsh, sorry, please don't take it personally."

"No, I understand, when would you be leaving?"

"Few weeks later."

My heart hammered in my chest. "What about your passport, you got it?"

"Yeah the guy from the office has been calling me for a long time; I'll collect it one of these days."

"Okay," I had to think about a new topic, I couldn't handle the awkward silence. "You know what I have started a little thing on facebook about......."

"I do know that," she interrupted tartly, "I have been reading, I don't know what are you upto?"

"Frankly even I don't know much, I had to do something after that day."

"Bye Harsh, I'll talk to you later."

"Bye," but she had already hung up. I shouldn't have reminded her about that day. I was sure what I was doing was the right thing to do, atleast for starters. I know it's easy to blame everyone around you, but harder to raise your voice and act. I wasn't doing exactly that, I know, but I had that in my mind eventually, I just had to figure out a way.

I kept the phone aside and tried sleeping.

But Nikita never allowed me to.

15

LITTLE MORE THAN A WEEK LATER…

I was looking for words to describe what I felt – ecstatic, stupefied, exhilarated, euphoric, astounded. I don't know, but I was definitely on cloud nine. *Was I dreaming?* I had to be. The past one week had been completely crazy, a multitude of comments kept pouring every day, every hour, every minute. I had a hard time replying to them. The likes rose like a hot balloon in the air. So many people were involved and talking about "The India I dream of."

Oh god this definitely was a dream!

The members on my page stood at a staggering 12,453 people now, the comments on my post about the list to be followed 5680 and the likes on this post were 10,785. That was a huge number for a few lines posted just ten days back. And the best part was people were thrilled, they were positive and had the intent to change themselves and others around them. Some of the comments sent me over the moon:

"Hey Harsh, I'm so glad you are doing this. Frankly I have always felt a bit guilty of not doing anything for my country other than complaining. Now I am; your list is wonderful for a start. I have stopped dumping waste on our roads, obey traffic rules religiously and I swear I would always vote. And that's not just me; I have made all my friends aware of your group and they are inspired too. Thanks for the initiative buddy!"

"We are all with you Harsh; you are doing a great job."

"I'm following all the points in your list and so are my friends; you are so right, stop complaining and do your part."

And I got an eight item to my list as well:

"Hi guys! All of you on this group, I have a question. Why do we people fight amongst each other for all the stupid reasons all the time? Why have we become so short tempered? We fight in queues, we fight on the roads, we fight in restaurants for petty issues, hell we even fight if someone has parked their car infront of our house. We have to stop that, if we still want to, it has to be against corruption, against unemployment and growing population. We are enough people on this group, let's all swear atleast we won't get in ugly spats for no reason. Harsh, I would really appreciate if you could put this on your list. Thanks a lot for getting us together."

You are welcome Chetna Deharia. That was from Bangalore. I was glad people were thinking and taking interest. It wasn't 'my thing' anymore. Everybody was getting involved from around the country. I had seen the profile of my visitors, they were from everywhere – North: Delhi, Punjab, Himachal Pradesh; East: Assam, Manipur, West Bengal; West: Gujarat, Maharashtra, even Goa and south: Kerala, Andhra Pradesh, Tamil Nadu. I could see people from different religions – Hindu, Muslim, Sikh and Christianity, people from all walks of life – students, housewives, teachers, doctors; even middle aged people were part of the page.

But that was not all; the blog I had posted last week got equal response and appreciation. There were 1480 comments already and over five thousand likes. It had become viral; people had become over enthusiastic about the idea. Even the blog had admirable comments. I could really see the power of internet now. Few days back it was only a little thought that had germinated in my mind. I had no clue what to do about it. Thanks to the internet and facebook, now I know.

If there were any doubts about the success of my little idea, it was cleared by Dev's call.

"Hey buddy," he sounded excited.

"Yeah Dev."

"I was looking at your group and blog, good going dude."

"Thanks," I replied tersely.

"Man, it's become a little rage of sorts."

"Not exactly, but yeah there are enough people following me now," I allowed myself a smile of pride when I said that.

"Good buddy, really," he hesitated a bit, "sorry for not taking it seriously before."

"Never mind Dev, you want to help now?" I really wanted someone to do some typing for me. There were so many comments pouring, I wanted someone to reply to them, not all but atleast the good ones. It was important to communicate regularly with my followers to maintain their morale.

"Sure man, I will, whatever you tell me."

"Okay," I said, now excited, "then come home tomorrow, we'll figure out what to do next."

"Okay sure, thanks, see you tomorrow, bye."

"Bye."

If Dev had become interested, then definitely it was good going. I wondered what Nikita would be thinking. I could bet that she would atleast be aware of this mania, if not interested. But she would never show it to me.

I was wrong as always!

Later that evening I got a call from her. I was astounded but elated; nevertheless, I picked it up.

"Hey Nikita," I couldn't feign my excitement.

"Hi Harsh." Her voice was still hollow.

"So glad you called, what's up?"

"Nothing much, how about you?"

"Everything is okay, pretty much the same." I didn't want to talk about what I was actually doing, that would annoy her and she would slam her phone right on my face like she did last time. I had learnt from my previous mistake and wasn't going to repeat it.

"You know I've been following your group and blog, they are doing unbelievably well."

"Oh you have?" That did take me by surprise. "Since when?"

"Right from the beginning, earlier I thought you were being stupid."

"And now?" I didn't let her complete her sentence.

"Actually it's come out quite well now, so many people are becoming interested, I must say Harsh I'm impressed, you are doing a great job."

"Thanks, thanks so much Nikita," I really needed that.

If absolutely anything would dissuade me from not doing this in the future, that statement of her would reinstate that.

"Sorry, I've been acting crazy all this while."

"No, no, absolutely not Nikita, I know what you have been through, I just want you to be happy."

"Thanks for understanding." She fell silent for a while, "so when can we all meet, it's been some time now."

"Yeah sure, whenever, let's meet up tomorrow, I'll tell Dev as well."

"Good, pick me up as you always do."

"I will, I definitely will." Those were the best times of my life. I would have woken up from my deepest slumbers to be her driver.

"Okay, bye and thanks for being my best friend."

Best friend? It didn't feel too good, but I guess I would remain a friend to her for the rest of my life. Best was only a euphemism.

"Sure, bye."

I hung up, it still felt nice. I never expected that call and ofcourse the fact that she wanted to meet. It could have been one of our last meetings. I felt a tad of pain as I had become so used to it now. But still somewhere, there lurked a tiny little desire to be with her. I knew I loved her and would have given up on anything in this world to have her.

Anything!

16

MAKE THE ASSHOLES FAMOUS!!!

I could not sleep the entire night and kept tossing on my bed awaiting the morning. I was finally going to meet Nikita. I was thrilled to say the least. Finally dawn broke and streaks of sunshine blazed into the corners of my room. I jumped from my bed lest I fell asleep now. I shaved after a couple of weeks as I had been busy earlier, took a shower and put on my best clothes. I reached her home two hours earlier. In my car, I kept dreaming and thought about all the topics that I would touch upon minus that night. Every minute passed like a year and it felt like an eternity waiting for her; perhaps that made it all the more special.

And then she came.

Wow! My lungs gasped for air. Breathing can get difficult at times.

She wore a light blue coloured long kurta which had some sort of embroidery over it; I didn't bother paying attention to that, dark blue skin fit jeans and glossy black pumps. Her hair was tied in a long and high ponytail, a pair of round silver earrings hung from her ears and her arms were emblazoned with a mosaic of multi-coloured bangles. They contrasted with each other and I wondered if she wore them just like that or worked on a steady pattern so it could match with one another. *How much patience does a girl have?*

"Hi," she said as she entered my car. She hugged me tight and so did I. It was the most marvelous thing I could have done with my life. Her scent intoxicated me and her soft hair bristled past my face. I could have been in that pose for years together.

"I missed you," she said as she retracted to her seat.

"Me too, you okay now?"

"Yeah, I'm trying to get over what happened." The melancholic tone of hers sent jitters inside me. "Forget it Harsh, I have to live with it, let's not talk about it."

"Hmm…." I nodded.

We didn't speak for the next ten minutes or so, just exchanged amicable glances. Whatever happened to all the topics I thought discussing with her! I was tongue-tied.

She finally spoke breaking the shackles of silence.

"Good job Harsh, I see you are being more patient while driving now, no honking, no screaming, you are even stopping at red lights."

"Yeah, well, as the age old adage goes practice what you preach, if I don't do it how can I expect others to do it?"

"Very good, I'm impressed."

I nodded.

"So there are a lot of members now huh, on your group."

"Yeah, they increase all the time."

"And what exactly are you guys upto?"

"Well we have kept it simple, nothing fancy, we all believe in changing our self first before expecting others to change."

"Good Harsh, it's a very nice thing you are doing, I must say I'm proud of you."

"Thanks, why don't you join our group?" I looked at her with refulgent eyes, "just hit the accept button and you'll be part of the community."

"I will, I surely will."

"I am sure you'll be a good follower."

"Ha, ha, I like your stuff Harsh, you have covered some real moot points, I don't mind applying them to my life, I know it makes sense."

"You do think that huh, good to know."

"Yeah, it's true; we complain all the time but never do anything about it."

"Wow, I'm happy you think likewise."

She put forth a benevolent smile. But even if she agreed with me, what difference it would make, she would be leaving in a few days time anyway.

"You know what Harsh, I guess you were right."

"Right? About what?"

"I don't feel like doing an MBA, I don't want to go that far, away from everybody, it'll be very difficult for me to concentrate. I have anyway had a rough last month; I can't do that to myself anymore. You were right, no country is perfect, that could have happened in America as well. I think I want to be here and be with you and help in what you are doing. I want to help you make a change. I believe in you belief."

Those words almost killed me in excitement, the first thing: she didn't want to go and secondly *she wanted to be with me.* Did she mean forever. *Was I dreaming or did she really say that?* What happened to her suddenly? All the hatred and anger vanished in thin air just like that. I did realize something that day – howsoever we pretend hating our country, a tiny little spot in our mind always remains which compels us to do something good for our great country. The same I guess had happened to Nikita. Well even if it wasn't true in her case, it was the best thing that happened to me since my birth.

"Really, you serious?" I tried feigning excitement with surprise.

"I know it's weird, but I have been doing a lot of thinking lately, I have actually done nothing myself then why do I complain all the time? I guess there's nothing wrong in our country, it's the people, so well yeah as you have been saying to the 15,000 members on your group, I want to do my part first."

I had no words; I felt a huge surge of emotions. They were motley of excitement, thrill, euphoria and a bit of surprise as well. But if Nikita was in it, then it had to become huge.

It did.

Few hours later, Dev grew a bit anxious on his seat. We were sitting at Barista, the Italian coffee giant in the Centre stage Mall in Saket – our favourite place on earth.

"So what can we do next?" he tugged at me.

We! So we were together again, only this time we had a goal, an ambition in life. That thing we said few years back in school about growing old together and dying infront of each other changed slightly. Now whenever we die presuming it would be atleast 40 years considering the statistics, we wanted to die in an improved India, a country where its people loved it and stood united for its betterment.

"Whatever we do it has to be simple and should make people believe in it and get them involved." I replied, logging to facebook on my computer. I had become a complete freak lately and carried it wherever I went. There were over 20,000 members on my group now and a plethora of comments greeted me. They were thank you notes, inspirational messages, few ideas et al. I had to read them all and reply to each one of them so that my followers would remain interested. But for now I had another important thing to do. I went to the 'about' section of my page and started typing. Now that Dev and Nikita were with me, it was about time I was more articulate about 'who we were':

"Welcome to 'The India I dream of'. This is a community by the Indians, for the Indians. We don't complain, grumble or criticize our country, but believe in doing our part for a better, safer and cleaner India. We don't make big changes, but believe in making small differences that eventually lead to big ones. We are patient and know that nothing happens overnight. We are all huge fans of the movie 'Rang De Basanti' and firmly believe that no country is perfect, it has to be made one."

"Here are a few things that we do and influence others around us too:"

And then I added my list of 8 points below.

"If you feel you are one of us, come join the community and let's together restore the lost pride. For starters you could share the link of this group page to your profile and let all your friends know about us.

P.S. – Be the change you want to see in the world"

Atleast now the strangers who visit our group would be aware what it is about and share it, that might just increase the traffic to the page.

"Hey, what if we make small cards about our page and distribute it to everyone here."

Nikita asked anxiously. I loved the 'our' part.

"No Nikita that won't be necessary, internet is our best bet for that, I just tell people to keep posting it on their profile which attracts enough people daily. The monumental increase in number is a testament to that." I replied.

"Yeah actually you are right, social networking at its best, huh."

"See Harsh, and remember few months back you were even hesitant to have an account on facebook, you should say thanks to me for that." Dev grinned through his pale yellow teeth.

"Yeah buddy thanks," I acknowledged.

"So what can we do next huh?" he asked.

"Take it easy Dev, it doesn't work that way, you can't be impatient, let facebook do its job of attracting people, we'll figure out what to do next in due course."

"Okay," he shrugged.

We sat there for about two more hours catching up for the times we missed since the last month. When Nikita grew solemn, we changed the topic.

"Come guys, let's go home now," I suggested. I had become more organized and cared about my time.

"Okay." They both got up.

The car ride back home was a silent one. Maybe it bought back old memories in Nikita's mind. We stopped at a red light at the Press Enclave road. Towards our left we could see the Qutub minar - the tallest minaret in India; a historical site where visitors flock every day. At the side of the road a guy was pissing – a common sight in India. I and Dev looked at each other in contempt; we had stopped doing that now. Behind, Nikita opened the back door and ran.

"Hey where are you going?" I screamed from the driver's seat.

"In a minute," she replied, without looking back.

We could see from the distance, she took out her mobile phone and started shooting 'the pissing guy'.

"Oh fuck, what the hell is she doing?" Dev laughed.

The guy sheepishly looked at Nikita, "hey what are you doing?" he hurriedly turned to the other side lest she and the camera caught a glimpse of *it*.

"You motherfuckers would never learn, can't you control your outburst to a nearby washroom."

"Okay, sorry but why are you shooting this?" He asked, bewildered with his back towards Nikita.

"See it in the news tomorrow."

"What?" The guy started running as fast as he could, away from Nikita, zipping up his pants. Nikita ran behind, still shooting him.

"Fuck you! Don't you ever do that again." she screamed from behind.

Meanwhile, the cars honked from behind. The signal had turned green and I was blocking the cars. Nikita emerged from behind, panting and we took off.

"Nikita what the hell were you doing?" We asked together in a paroxysm of laughter, "you are crazy."

"Nothing, instinct may be, just happened at the spur of the moment," she replied casually.

"What?" Dev was still laughing.

I wasn't. I pondered; maybe I got my next idea. "Hey just a thought, what if we make the guy famous."

I got puzzled looks from Dev and Nikita.

"No I mean what if we put that on the internet; you know facebook or maybe youtube."

Still puzzled looks!

"You know so many people can see that then," I continued talking more to myself now.

"So how would that help anyway?" Dev asked with stolid indifference.

"I mean let's make the guy famous on the internet and let's start this practice with others too, maybe that would deter them from doing it." I said a bit doubtful. *Was I even listening to what I said!*

"Yeah and maybe we could add the link of the video on youtube to our group page and ask our 20,000 members to share it on their profile, who knows the guy I just shot might turn out to be one of their friends. Just imagine how embarrassing it will be for him, atleast that would make sure he doesn't do it again"

I accorded with Nikita, she was right. With so many members on the group now, the world was getting small. Maybe I could tell all others on our group to do it too— make the assholes famous. And it won't be restricted to only people pissing in the open but similar unethical acts that would include but not be limited to people spitting or maybe throwing garbage, disobeying traffic rules – we could get a picture of their number plate in that case, people fighting over petty issues on the roads, lazy and pesky government servants, cops taking bribes and thousands of other uncivilized acts. Hell, yeah, now it was making sense. I shared the idea with Dev and Nikita.

"Yeah it sounds cool, make the assholes famous," Dev replied.

"And the members on our group increase all the time; imagine if everyone is shooting assholes like these and putting it on the internet, how many of them are we talking about, and considering the reach of facebook I'm sure those videos would reach the respective actors somehow." I said now a bit clear of my initial thought.

"And imagine the look on their face when they see a public broadcast of their puerile acts." Nikita said, laughing.

"You are right Nikita," I replied, "that would deter them from repeating it and maybe all others who see it. Who knows when a camera is being pointing at them? Everyone carries a smart phone these days, so nobody has to worry about carrying a camera really."

"Right!"

I bade them goodbye after dropping them to their respective places. I had a massive urge for a leak during the drive back home. I controlled it. I had to; who knows someone had a camera in their hands, ha!

When I reached home, I logged back to facebook and put a little post on my group page about our new plan. I put the following heading:

"MAKE THE ASSHOLES FAMOUS"

And then I went for a pee.

In my washroom!

17

ANOTHER WEEK LATER.....

I was euphoric and so were Dev and Nikita. We were sitting at Dev's place, back to our Sunday routine. And we had two reasons to be monumentally cheerful. First, our group had more than fifty thousand members now, 52485 to be precise. I had no idea about the number of comments on our group page, but on an average we figured out atleast one comment a minute did get posted.

And secondly, "MAKE THE ASSHOLES FAMOUS" post had received 6756 likes and there were 3885 comments floating under it. It seems people had loved the idea completely. They were in total agreement with us and shared similar thoughts that it *would* work. Some of them even spoke about buying new phones which had better cameras. What was testament to the belief were the hundreds of videos posted on you tube already and their links shared on so many profiles. They were people urinating, spitting, throwing trash, people fighting over menial issues – one of these videos was over 10 minutes and the person posting it had done a fabulous job by recording their close up pictures. There were some videos on the roads as well about people blocking free turns, taking U-turns where it was prohibited – hell so many car numbers were displayed on you tube already. I'm sure their owners would have watched them with disdain. In a way we were also helping the cops.

Some of them had even clicked pictures in government offices of employees sleeping and lazing around; attention was also given to their name tags and ranks being clearly visible. *Wow! That was commendable!* There were so many comments posted under the videos as well and some of them already had over a thousand views. I guess time wasn't far when people had to watch out for their actions lest it got captured and displayed.

I kept motivating people with my comments and appreciated their work. Considering the population of India, fifty grand was still a measly number. There was so much scope for improvement. But having said that our group had become famous and excited people! It was like a damn stampede on our group page, so many people were writing now and getting involved, there was so much enthusiasm, excitement and positive vibes on the page. Strangers had gotten together and discussed about the betterment of the society. I even got advises to increase my list.

I did.

There were three more items added to my list. It was the following:

"9. What is with the 'Indian standard time' tag that we people are so unmistakably proud of? We actually take pride in not being punctual. Be it office, college, meetings, hell even the Commonwealth games for that matter. And it's something the entire world is aware of. A profession like mine proffers visits to a lot of countries and I can swear we get to hear about our vice from varying nationalities with umpteen disgust. We are scoffed at and not taken seriously. It's not something to be proud of but rather get rid of. I'm sure it's no big deal to work on a menial thing as this. So the next time you have given a time for a meeting, even a date for that matter, be ethical and always wear a watch.

10. This is something we Indians should be ashamed of - eve teasing, rapes and harassment of women. We have no right to be proud of our culture and background when women are still looked down upon in most places. It might come as a surprise but even in places like Delhi a girl child is treated with disdain. Are we ever going to improve? It is a well known fact that women are doing equally well as men in every field nowadays.

And what about eve-teasing! Well I won't say I have done that but seriously I have had my lascivious glares at women, embarrassing them. This goes out for all the guys out there. Stop doing it, but if you still want to, then have the balls to ask her out first.

11. I guess a little bit of statistics will be good to make you understand my next concern. Tourism brings over 6% of India's Gross Domestic Product. But we don't care about that, do we? I have seen so many times foreigners are taken for a ride in our country, they are not treated with respect, cornered and treated as outsiders and well white women, I don't need to say anything about that. Do we really want to lose

that much money and lose respect from the rest of the world? I am sure none of us wants that, so guys please next time you see a foreigner around, be courteous and humble, show them what we have got and why this is a great country for ages."

I was having a wonderful time posting my feelings. Never before was I really heard and by so many people at the same time. I was sure in the next 24 hours more than fifty grand people would have read that and shared their thoughts about the same. How cool was that? I guess facebook was really a panacea for all that was buried inside me for a long time. Thanks to it, my feelings were getting surfaced.

There was one more feeling though that I wanted to surface.

My heart thumped.

18

ANOTHER IDEA…

Barely a month into the act and I felt like a winner already. I wouldn't say I had made an enormous change but the very fact that I made people to think and act was a feeling far from satisfying. I had never felt like that in years. Even my professional life didn't conjure this amount of gratification; personal life didn't even qualify for a comparison.

Nikita had left her job now; Dev wasn't much interested in cheating his customers either. So that got us together every day. We pondered all day, introspected new ideas that would continually improve our little endeavour. Having said that, I guess it was far from being little now! The number had reached the 6 figure mark, I officially had more than 1 lakh members who lauded and appreciated my initiative and above all the idea that bought so many people together. None of us believed in doing something huge, but changing our self and others around us. It was working and I could see that. So many people were being introduced to the group, so many links shared, my comments receiving thousands of likes and appreciative comments. But above all the whole vibe of the group was a very positive one unlike it is in our country for an act of such bearing. Even the Anna Hazare campaign had so many critics, but so far all of us believed in each other.

Even my blogs attracted a lot of traffic as I posted its link on my group page. I had posted about three more blogs after the first one. In one of them I had written that no country is perfect. I had illustrated that with statistics, about corruption even in the developed countries of the world. Ours was still developing so there wasn't any need really to mull over the corruption and poverty in our country. It had received more than two thousand comments. I think we Indians are very gullible, if an opinion is presented with a well researched truth, everyone buys it. Although I won't say I was trying to misguide people but I guess before people really do something they should believe that it would bear results. No one likes to change unless something good is in the pipeline.

My next blog was about the development and how our country had evolved in the last twenty years. Again I backed it up with a powerful research. Here people were again made to believe that India is improving, however slow but it is in the right direction. Considering the fact that it's just been a little over sixty years since our Independence, we guys have done a good job. I wanted people to feel good about our country; a few riffs here and there can't take away the fact that we are on our way to becoming a developed country. Slowly but steadily! That got me a little over three thousand comments.

It was like quid pro quo, the people who read my blogs were directed towards our group and those on our group towards the blog. That worked as a catalyst for a monumental rise in my visitors.

It was a balmy Friday afternoon when another idea hit us. We sat on the roof top of the Select Citywalk mall that offered a panoramic view of South Delhi. It was an open place with bright coloured canopies above us to protect us from the scorching sunlight. There were hordes of people around us shopping and reveling in the multitudinous brands that spanned across the entire mall. We sipped our coffee slowly and were thinking. I had my laptop on and was scrolling through the various comments.

"Wow man, a lakh people already," Dev blurted as he had a look through the corner of his eyes.

"It's just the beginning dude," I said with a shade of pride.

"I guess Harsh, we could still do a lot better," Nikita muttered, "there are so many people of our age group in India, I'm sure atleast half of them would be on facebook."

"Yeah you are right Nikita, but I guess it's going to take a while before we have all the people onboard, isn't? Maybe few months, I reckon," I replied sipping my coffee. "Patience is the key baby."

"You know I was wondering what if a time comes where at any time around us we have enough members and we can talk to them, discuss new ideas, take their point of view, and also what if someone is in trouble at some point of time and he wants help, that person could summon all the people around him and........."

I didn't let Nikita complete her sentence. "Nikita you are crazy, you know India is such a huge country, our members would be scattered all over, how could you possibly think of that working?"

Nikita pondered for a moment, "hey just think maybe a year from now you might have
over ten lakh members, what if we all come together to help each other out."

"Nikita what are you even saying?" Dev countered this time.

"Okay, let's look at it this way, I'm on the road and a bunch of guys are trying to act funny with me, you know eve-teasing, like it happens all the time. I want help, so what do I do? I can't call the cops, they are idiots, they give a damn anyway, the bystanders would just watch and have fun; they wouldn't be of much help as well. So what I could do is call upon our group and some of the people who would be around me at that instant could come out to help me."

"Nikita you are insane, how could that be possible, you think anybody would care or rather have the time for this?"

"Exactly my point, not now, but once we have enough people we would take a resolution, a vow maybe that everyone has to step up and help."

The idea didn't make me wildly interested, but there was just a bit of sense in what she said. I logged on to the father of search engines – google.com. I typed 'total area of India". It was close to 30 lakh square kilometers, I learnt a few seconds later. Then I typed 'Indians on facebook'. The number was around 3 crores as of June 2011. So for every one square kilometer in India there are only 10 people on facebook and that too scattered all over the country excluding the villages, ofcourse. But more importantly, there was no way that all of them would be on our group even in the distant future, howsoever optimistic I got.

Nikita's gaze widened at me. "See I told you," she shrieked.

"Told me what?" I sniffed, "still there'll be what? We don't have that many people on our group now and even if we had I'm not sure that would work."

"Harsh wait," Nikita countered, "what if I call you tomorrow and say that one of my friends is in a problem few kilometers away, say three or maybe four, won't you go and help?"

"Depends on how hot she is," Dev replied through a mouthful of lust. It was amazing it didn't even take him a second to reply to that.

"Fuck you psycho, I'm not talking to you," she grunted at him, then looked back at me, "come on Harsh tell me, would you or would you not?"

"Yeah, I would, but...."

"Shut up, so you got my point," she interjected, "then why all others on the group cannot do so; let's say if someone wants help for anything, they post it on the group page and since nowadays almost everybody uses net on their phone, they would get a message instantly and if they are within a reach of say 3 kilometers, it would be their duty to stop whatever they are doing and rush for help."

"I guess we could try that, what say Harsh?" Dev asked.

"Okay, if you guys insist, we'll give it a shot," I had to concede, Nikita would have killed me otherwise. Frankly I was not much in favour of that, it sounded too good to be true. Perhaps Nikita had got a bit too enthusiastic. This idea might just work if we had an enormous number of members on our group, or perhaps all the Indians on facebook, but with just about a lakh of them. Boy, I had serious doubts.

Together we framed the following lines:

"Let's be united and stand for each other – Here's a new plan guys. All of us have smart phones these days, we use internet on the phone more than on our computers. For those of you who don't please do it, for this plan to succeed all of you have to be involved. The idea is pretty simple, like it always is – if any one of us happens to be in trouble, it could be anything, say you are being pestered in a government office, or by a traffic cop, you get in a fight with rowdy strangers, if a girl is being harassed, anything else for that matter, post it immediately on this group page including the address of your whereabouts. Every one of us would get a message on our mobile phone and then let's all vow that we would rush for help if it is happening near to us, let's say 3-4 kilometers. I'm sure we can do atleast this much for our fellow countrymen.

Let's get together in our little fight against the menace in our society.

Any suggestions and comments welcome. Do share your opinions!

P.S. – Be the change you want to see in the world."

Nikita pressed 'enter' and there it was. Somehow I found this idea a bit weird, I wasn't sure if this would really work.

Do we Indians have so much time for each other? Would we really care to help?

I guess the answer was in the question!

19

IT DOES WORK....

Less than twenty four hours later, I got the following post on our group page:

"Hey Harsh, I am Rajiv from Bombay, a huge fan of yours who follows all your thoughts and religiously follows them. I want to thank you for the idea that you posted yesterday. It has really helped me.

It was around ten last night. I was sitting in my car with my girlfriend whom I intend to marry next year. There were some issues which we were trying to address. We were not drunk, nor were we physically engaged, my car was not parked in a 'No parking' area. A man in a khaki uniform knocked hard at my window pane. I thought he was drunk and he started barking, forcing me to come out. I obliged not sure what wrong had I done. He ushered me away from my car towards another stolid faced police man. Both spoke to me with sheer despise, they asked for my license, car papers which I submissively handed over to them. Then I was told to come with them to a nearby police station. That startled me and I asked reason for the same as I was not doing anything illegal. They rudely asked about who the girl was in the car, where does she live, who all lives with her. And then I got a shock of my life when they started abusing me and her and said that don't fool us, we know that she's a prostitute. I was alarmed and requested them to believe me. I knew there wasn't any point retaliating, so I had to be polite. This went on for the next few minutes. I begged them to let us go and return my documents. But they persisted and continued abusing and yelling. Then it occurred to me of throwing money at them. To my dismay they gleefully accepted it. I excused myself saying that my wallet was in the car. They kept an eye on me from behind. As I was walking, your idea suddenly dawned on me. In the car I immediately posted for help on this page from my phone. To be honest I was not sure if I would get any help. I did try to kill time by futile arguments with them hoping that somebody would turn to help me. And to my consternation, in the next ten minutes, four people turned up. I told them the entire story and how those cops were trying to make money out of me for no reason. They confronted the cops and told them they were my friends and they knew the girl, how could they badger me like that? One of them took out his phone and started shooting the entire conversation and threatened them of putting it on the internet. Another one said he knows the DIG of the region and he would complain about them. I guess they were petty officers and that was enough to terrify them. They apologized and disappeared without any trace. I thanked the four guys for their time and effort.

So I am the first person who has tried your remarkable idea and dude it works, it's just that you have to be lucky to have people around you. I like to thank you for your efforts and initiative. This group rocks!

And for fellow readers, next time you are in trouble, do post it on this page and trust me help would be on its way soon. Believe in this idea, it has worked for me and so will it for you."

Wow! That was tremendous. He had actually posted the link of the video that was shot last night. I clicked on it and was directed to youtube. There I could see two paltry looking cops being confronted by these guys. That video had already received over a thousand views. So 'make the assholes famous' worked in tandem with this idea. It was overwhelming to see the people's response. They had actually made good use of my ideas, rather our ideas. Nikita would be elated to know that her idea worked. I called her up to tell about it, but she was already on the page and had seen it. She did condescend to me as I didn't believe in it earlier. But we laughed over it. I was so glad Nikita was a part of this. Without her, I guess I would have lost interest in this sometime in the near future. But now that she was with me, I felt so strong and rejuvenated.

Few hours later, there was another post:

"Hi everybody, I am Priyesh Tandel from Baroda. I am the latest fan of this idea that was posted yesterday. I was in a national bank yesterday in my city. I had to get a demand draft made in favour of Mumbai University as I had to apply for a course. I reached the bank early in the morning as everybody knows how lazy these people in a government office are. But that much lazy, I wasn't aware. I had been in the bank for two hours, deposited the money, submitted the form to a middle aged, bald man at the counter and he had told me to wait for a few minutes. Two hours later and I was still waiting. I asked him how much more time would it take. He gave me all lame excuses, told me the computer is down, there is so much work, some pending issues need to be resolved and wait for a little more while. What annoyed me was the fact that he had time for three cups of tea, ranting on the phone, gossiping with his fellow employees, but for my work which would have taken maybe two minutes, he couldn't put his lazy ass to work. I waited for another hour and then I don't know why I just posted it on the page – 'tormented by a stupid bank official, please help' and I wrote the address beneath. In just about fifteen minutes, I had two guys and two girls with me. Together we snubbed the bald man, complained to the manager of the bank; one of the girls took pictures of the man and told him 'we will make you famous asshole, check out your pictures on the internet.' That embarrassed the man and within a minute my draft was ready. I guess these people have to be taught to do their work; they have taken things for granted as they work in a government office, it is perceived, they would never get sacked.

Hey, thanks a lot Harsh, for this wonderful platform that you have created, it has made all of us come together. I am so grateful to you for this and so is every other person on this group. I'm sure together we can improve our country in bits and pieces.

To all you guys out there, let's stand up and help each other out, but first let's change our self."

And there in the bottom he attached links of the pictures. Wow, *assholes* were really getting famous, I thought. There were plenty of videos and pictures from all over India already on youtube which included uncivilized and unethical citizens, government officials, corrupt traffic policemen, rowdy men harassing women, people disobeying traffic rules, petty fights. People had got used to the idea; any boorish behaviour was being recorded and shared with so many people. Internet had made the world a really small place; with links being shared on so many profiles, I'm sure the people who were shot would have sheepishly seen themselves on youtube as well. If nothing else, atleast the disgrace it would have brought them would have made them change. That was the beauty of this idea. And well now, people were even ready to help each other out. I guess there is a lot of agony in everyone's hearts, against the system, our government and the people. Everyone wants to contribute in whatever way they can; I had just shown them the way.

We Indians are very good people, it's just that we lack the ability to take initiative. We like following the path that has been laid for us. But once we are on the right track, we religiously follow it. Now that everybody knew what they could do to be a part of the change, everyone was contributing. There was no bias here, no political divide, no religion or caste; we were all one – an average Indian who wanted this country to change by doing their part. I could see the enthusiasm of the people, not many times had I seen more than a lakh Indians get united for a cause.

I so loved Mark Zuckerberg and his facebook!

Over the next few days, the three of us were very busy. The number of my fans had risen to over two lakhs now. We were getting enormous amounts of comments and suggestions. I made sure to reply to each one of them. People from all over the country were interacting with each other. There were over a hundred posts already about help being summoned by distressed people, some of them even in areas like Kota in Rajasthan, Gorakhpur in Uttar Pradesh where there is internet access; thank you notes followed them. Atleast a dozen videos of 'assholes' were posted daily on youtube and our group page now, flustered people hiding their faces from cameras, grunting and wobbling all over; people in uniforms, number plates of cars et al.

It had become a rage. I guess partly due to the novelty of the idea and partly due to the hidden desire in so many people to do good for the community. I continued writing my blogs inspiring and motivating people to participate for the cause. They were getting famous too, I could see that. Every blog of mine received not less than three thousand comments and almost three times the views. Awesome would have been an understatement.

Slowly things were changing, but we still had a long way to go.

Really long!

20

THE MAGAZINE - THE INDIA
I DREAM OF...

One month later!

THE number read 12, 47, 856! There was little more than a six hundred percent rise in the number of our members. It was crazy, I had lost track of the number of comments that kept pouring up every minute on the page. I had stopped replying to them anymore, now that I could see the motivation emblazoned in their words. I was no more a leader now, but a follower of my own thoughts and ideas like the twelve lakh people on my group.

There was a cohesive bond among us all on the group. A little thread of patriotism tied us together. We were all helping out each other in dreary times, Nikita's idea bore fruits, the seeds of which had been planted just a few weeks ago. Everybody was involved, there were die hard fanatics on the group now who wrote much more than I ever did. Youtube had over a thousand 'asshole' videos. It was no more a little thing on the internet. It had become huge.

The best was my blog. Since there were so many people viewing and talking about it on a daily basis, I got offers from companies who wanted to advertise their products on my blog. I gleefully accepted them. Shoes, shirts, gifts, baby care and various other products enticed my viewers. I wasn't really losing anything by sharing a part of my space with these companies. On the contrary, I was being paid big bucks. So much that I decided to quit sailing. Like Nikita, even I didn't want to leave this country. I wanted to be here and continue this uprising, perhaps fortify it. The blogs had made me financially sustainable, so what was the need to work anyway!

We three continued meeting everyday; discussing and sometimes enjoying our self; reveling in the respect and popularity we got. We had posted our pictures on the group page under the 'photos' section two weeks back. It was Dev's idea; he believed it would be a good way to lure girls. I don't know how much that worked, but sometimes we did draw a lot of public attention. People had started recognizing us and once we even got applause from a few college kids who first confirmed our identity. I never thought this would bring us fame, nevertheless it was welcome.

Those days there was another thing that we were thinking about. One of our fans from the group had suggested us to start a magazine. We had our doubts about it; that was way beyond our league. Social networking was a relatively simple task; this one needed a lot of professionalism. We didn't even have the slightest of clues of even starting one, forget running it.

Late into a Saturday evening, we were drinking at Dev's house. His parents were out of town, so that seemed to be a perfect destination for a night out. Some of the best decisions in life are made under the influence of alcohol, this was one of them.

"I don't know guys, how would be able to do it?" Dev stuttered. Alcohol had completely taken over his mind.

"Tell you what, I really think we should do it, it'll be amazing to be a publisher of a fucking magazine guys!" Nikita crooned in an alcoholic haze.

"Yeah, right but how would be go about it," I replied. I guess I was the most sober among the three of us.

"Let's ask our father then, google.com." Dev suggested.

Over the next hour we did a little research on 'how to start a magazine in India'. We found out about the initial investment involved, registration of the magazine, application forms, documents required, approximate time taken for approvals and other expenditures. It wasn't that difficult, we *could* do that.

"Okay one question," Nikita blurted still looking at the computer screen, "what the hell would we be writing about?"

"Ha!" I sneered, "Welcome to my world sweetie, that's exactly what I have been thinking."

And then again, we had a few more drinks and racked our brains harder.

"Hey I have a suggestion." Dev peered at us.

"Fuck you Dev, there's only one thing you can think of." Nikita rejected him outright and so did I.

"Guys atleast listen," he pleaded, "can't we do what we have been doing with our group."

"Do what man?" Either the alcohol was strong or Dev was an irritating asshole. Or both!

"What I mean is that all this while it's been a collective effort right, everybody is contributing on our group page, everybody is changing themselves, everybody is helping, so why not this? See we could tell these people about the magazine and ask them to contribute in this as well."

"Okay and," I was all ears now; there was a shade of sense in it, not much though.

"And perhaps they could write articles or anything about the country with similar theme, maybe someone is being harassed by a public servant or someone has been denied justice, social issues and blah, blah, blah; in short anything that deserves an attention. We'll choose the best articles, maybe modify it and then publish it. It'll be like 'make the assholes famous' theme, only thing this would be in print. See now whatever reach we have it's only through the net and only to people using facebook, but this way we could be interacting with thousands of other people who are not net savvy, see my point guys."

I ruminated for a little while.

"Thank you Dev," I said appreciatively, "you have made a lifetime of sense in a day."

"Really Dev," Nikita said in addendum, "it does make sense; I didn't expect this from you."

And then as an afterthought we held our glasses tight and gulped down the brown coloured liquid. *Bottoms up!*

We put the idea on our group page and waited for everybody's response. It didn't matter much though, as we had made our mind of doing it anyway. It was more to tell everybody of our new plan and perhaps draw out a few suggestions.

"Hello fellow Indians. A hearty congratulation to all of you for the figure has reached over a million now. I do believe people from all the 28 states and 7 union territories of our great country are part of this rebellion now. Maybe I'm being too optimistic very soon, but I have already started seeing results – I see a cleaner India, a more cooperative bustle around me all the time. Our hard work has started paying off guys; we need to keep that up. Winds of change are slowly but steadily blowing in the country!

There's another thing I wanted to talk to you guys about. We are planning to start a magazine from next month. It will be called 'The India I dream of". I want every one of you to contribute to it. Any idea, suggestions, complaints, grudges or grievances to be addressed to theindiaIdreamof@gmail.com. We would pick out the articles needing immediate attention and publish them. This will be another of our effort to address those issues which seldom get any notice. Remember it does not necessarily have to be your own story, if you see any injustice around you, anything that requires attention; you shouldn't keep quiet and wail over it, rather report. Remember, this country would become better not only if 'assholes' improve, but also if good and well meaning Indians like us realize our responsibilities and take action. I pledge all of you to pull up your socks and let's together fight the mess in our society.

Regards,

Harsh

P.S. – Be the change you want to see in INDIA."

We did all the requisite work in the coming days, the comments on my last post had enthused me beyond all limits. I had become a national hero, it seems. People were all praises for me; one of them actually said I should be nominated for the Padma Bhusan award – the third highest civilian award in the country after Bharat Ratna and Padma Vibhushan. Spare it guys, this was just the beginning. We still have a long way to go, I thought.

Our mail box was flooded. The three of us had to really burn the midnight lamp to catch up with it, deciding which one would make it to the magazine was even tougher. Some of them were brilliant stories deserving the limelight.

We had decided the first issue of our magazine wouldn't be too flashy. There would be a few big articles; the ones we reckon require the maximum attention, a couple of short stories, then some facts about the Indian growth story. Through this part we wanted to introduce a feel good factor among us Indians. I actually wanted to show the people we are not doing too bad as many perceive it to be. I wanted to talk about our growing economy, decrease in illiteracy and unemployment rates, decrease in poverty levels, emergence of the Indian middle class and their disposable incomes, about the billionaires, actors, sportsmen, musicians who have earned worldwide respect. In short I wanted people to feel good about our country and inculcate a certain amount of respect in them. In addition I wanted to write about the shams, corruption, recession, et al in the developed countries of the world. The idea was pretty simple again – no country is perfect, it has to be made one.

We braced our self for all the research that had to be done to make our magazine erudite and entertaining at the same time. As for the entertainment, another brilliant idea had hit us. It seems we had fallen in love with the word 'asshole'. This idea too was about that. We had coined a section which was called 'Top 10 assholes of the month.' Here we thought of maligning all those people who were a menace to the society; we knew we would have hundreds of them, but only the most deserving would have the honour of being on that *revered* list!

It wasn't very difficult choosing the big articles for our first month. All three of us were in agreement which ones it would be. They had caught our attention the moment we read about them. The first one was from a journalist from Madhya Pradesh. The lady who had sent us the mail appeared to be in her mid twenties and I could tell from her pictures that she had sent along with the story, she was pretty. She had given a little introduction about herself first. She worked for a local newspaper in a place called Besaria in Bhopal district. She too like us, she had said, wanted to make a change in the society. We read her story together:

"The Public distribution system or PDS as it is called was established by the government of India to distribute subsidized food and non- food items to the under privileged sections of the society. But as we all know owing to a lot of corruption and as it is channelized through a lot of sections, it barely manages to reach the needy. Here in Dillod village in Besaria about 40 kilometres from Bhopal, there is a lot of deceit and inspite of a lot of struggle from our team, absolutely nothing has changed. The PDS dealers are selling food grains at a price higher than the government fixed rates to make profits and the poor have no choice but to buy them. Other than that these dealers replace the good quality products with inferior stock that is often expired and damaged. The good quality items then go to merchants who sell them at a much higher price in the open market. This is atleast thrice the price of what they actually procure from the government. There is absolutely no accountability and a lot of government officials and public servants make huge profits at the account of the poor. This has led to malnutrition and people are dying from hunger but nobody wants to take any responsibility.

We had approached the block development officer and written to the sub-divisional magistrate (SDM) as well about the inefficiency of the system and the deceit of the PDS dealers. Few weeks later when the SDM came to our village, we approached with a public petition signed by more than 400 people of the village. He assured he would take some action against the dealers, however weeks have passed but still nothing has changed. Death threats are given to us by the dealer's men and they have warned us to keep out of this.

Hence I'm writing to you so as to expose the people behind this. With your popularity and the reach of your magazine I'm sure this won't fall on deaf ears. Kindly publish this story in your magazine so that justice can be sought and poor people can get their right.

Best regards,

Shikha"

The next story was about the corruption in Mahatma Gandhi National Rural Employment Guarantee Act (MGNREGA) program. There is a small village Bishala in Barmer district near Jodhpur, Rajasthan. A social activist Mohan Awasthi had sent us the details about the problems faced by the villagers:

The NREGA program aims at enhancing the livelihood security of people in rural areas by guaranteeing 100 days of wage- employment in a financial year to a rural household whose adult members volunteer to do unskilled manual work. However as is always the case, this scheme is beset with controversies owing to corrupt officials and lack of accountability. People have to sometimes bribe the officials to get a job and a job card, something that is their right under this program as required by the Central Government. At other times people are made to work without any wages. As per this program, workers are to be paid within 15 days of each fortnight's work being completed. However people here have to wait months to get their hard-earned wages.

There are other instances where there is 'fictitious' work and fake job cards are issued to people who do not exist. In this process, money is withdrawn from the Central Government but that never reaches the poor. I along with few other activists have been fighting for the rights of the villagers for the past year without any results.

We took these labourers to the Gram Sevak (Village development officer) but he ignored us saying you go to the post office. Over there, we were told to go to the Gram Sevak. Even the site supervisor was indifferent to our petitions. Everybody is passing the buck and blaming others.

We tried meeting the District Program Coordinator to voice our concern, but they are too busy or perhaps indifferent to listen to us. All the officials involved in this are making huge money and the poor continue to work without any wages. Kindly publish the story in your magazine to spread some awareness. That might just bring the people here some justice.

Warm Regards,
Mohan"

There were few other articles that were part of the first issue of our magazine. These included bribes paid by civilians to get a birth certificate, marriage certificate, passport address verification; government officials pestering people in national banks, RTOs, public offices, passport offices, et al.

In the 'Top 10 assholes of the month' we managed selecting 10 guests, though we had a lot of options from the thousands of recommendations we got from our fans. In all of them, the one thing common was the clarity of their picture; they had to become famous after all. Their name, details, the city which was graced by their presence and all other paraphernalia pertaining to them was scrupulously displayed beneath the respective articles. Apart from this, the link on youtube which had their video was also attached; for all people who still hadn't seen it, could have a laugh. Some of the assholes included were:

The cop of Mumbai who had called Rajiv's girlfriend a prostitute and unnecessarily harassed them! He was found guilty of being unprofessional and for ignominy of the police department of this country.

The bank official of Baroda who took more than 3 hours to issue a demand draft, a work that should have taken barely 15 minutes.

Our first victim, the guy who was pissing near the Qutub Minar was also in the list. Atleast that would stop all the leaking penis hanging out in the open! I was so glad Nikita had not shot me or Dev doing that.

But the last one, to be honest, me and Nikita were assholes because we declared Dev one. Ha! That was hilarious. We had kept Dev privy to all the information that would be published in the magazine; however we changed this last asshole at the last moment.

"This one is for all the girls out there. Have a look at this picture closely, this guy could be a doctor, a cricketer, a space scientist, captain, model; but trust us he is none. He will lure you by his good looks and boyish charms, but don't get enticed, don't get caught in the trap of his flirtatious nature. Girls who find a date on facebook, beware, that's his repertoire, fascinating you through his cheeky one-liners."

We had been so kind not to include his name and any other details, but that was it, we couldn't have done anything more, he was an asshole in the true sense.

If we were criticizing people, we should appreciate some as well, we collectively thought. India is a land of varying personalities. This thought led us to include another article in our magazine: "Top 10 Indians of the month". This list would not include any celebrities or already successful people, we were sure of that; but those who constantly make an effort to selflessly contribute to the society and help people in distress. This idea was addressed few days back on our group page and the people were unanimously in favour of it. Again we handpicked the most deserving candidates for the list. Some of them were:

There is an old lady in Dehradun, we had read through one of our fans based in that city, who runs a little school for poor children. A group of 15-20 children visit her house everyday in the morning. She serves them tea and breakfast and then together with her daughter and sometimes son in law teaches them late in the afternoon after which she serves lunch. All for free! She doesn't care how would it be helping the country grow, how is it improving the society, but just carries out her moral obligations responsibly. The neighbours of the old woman help her in whatever little way they can by contributing for food, money and sometimes time.

A doctor in the city of Rourkela in Orissa finds 2 hours every day after his job to provide free selfless service to the poor who can't afford hospitals. He also provides them medicines at subsidized rates.

A gentleman in Bangalore runs an old age home that provides food and shelter to the displaced and helpless senior citizen. Some of them are poor while others are abandoned by their children. It has accommodation for close to 100 people.

Apart from the three articles, two contrasting lists, facts and figures about our country and others, there was one huge thing we were missing – the editorial note. We framed the following lines:

"India is a land of diverse cultures, religions, languages and well, corruption. Corruption has impregnated deep in the society and each one of us some way or the other, directly or indirectly has been affected by it. In this magazine, we won't bother publishing issues that don't affect us directly, like the 1,76,000 crore 2G scam, Adarsh housing and the commonwealth scam, but everyday being asked to bribe, dealing with corrupt government officials does. We are here to fight that, for the others we have our government, judiciary and police to take care. We take up those cases which go unnoticed most of the time due to the power of the corrupt.

Sure the above mentioned scams do affect us as we are being robbed of humongous amounts of money, but somehow it does not make much of a difference to the lives of the common man. Here we publish stories that bother us on a day to day basis. We are not here to fight corruption but to ensure we do not encourage it. Fighting corruption is the prerogative of the government or well,

Anna Hazare's. We are here only to ensure we get our well deserved rights as a citizen of this country.

We urge all of you to contribute to our articles by writing to us at theindiaIdreamof@gmail.com. This has to be a combined effort by us and you, the readers. Any story deserving attention to be brought to our attention and we assure you it will be covered in our subsequent issues.

In addition there is a column "Top 10 assholes of the month" and "Top 10 Indians of the month". We request you to help us find the most suitable candidates for both the above categories. I'm sure there will be many around, keep sending us as many as you can find and we'll pick the most deserving candidates for the same. Do remember to send us their photographs or videos, their names, locality and city. The idea is to make them famous!

One last thing – do join the group - "The India I dream of" on facebook and be a part of the change that is forthcoming in India."

The 11 points which were on my facebook group also found the space on the next page after the editorial. I requested all those who read the magazine to sincerely follow those and also motivate all others around them to follow.

And with that, our magazine was ready to storm the market. We hired a reputed magazine distributor who had well established distribution centres in quite a few cities of India. Also, they had a good network of customers across the country including organized retail chain stores. We initially planned of our magazine's availability in few cities such that it would have its reach in the entire country.

The price of our magazine was a measly ten bucks so that no one had a second though before buying it. I wanted more people to be aware of it first before I start making profits. And well the money it would generate would surely be huge. But I had already planned what I was going to do with the money.

I had to practice what I preach!

21

THE INTERVIEW

ABOUT a week after the magazine was published, we could see that it was doing exceptionally well. Our distributor kept us pestering for more copies. There was one very obvious reason for it's phenomenal success - close to 15 lakh members on the group were aware of it due to its advertising on facebook and since so many of them had contributed in it, the sales were bound to be a lot.

I had a discussion with Dev and Nikita about the money being generated through this. They had left the decision to me. I was clear of two things; firstly the money generated would be used to expand the reach of the magazine. Not only did I want it to reach as many cities and towns of the country, I also wanted it to be published in all the languages of the country. I didn't want language to be a barrier. And secondly a part of the money earned would be used for the welfare of the under privileged people of the society. I didn't want to be a philanthropist, so for the time being I set the amount as ten percent of my net earnings.

With that I added another point to my list making it twelve:

"For your information, more than seventy percent of India's population lives on less than twenty rupees a day. Such a shame, isn't it? We have decided to shell out a ten percent of our earnings for this cause, it will not make a big difference, but atleast it's good for a start. We will be putting our money in a well meaning NGO so it can be used for the upliftment of the poor. I request you all to be a bit generous and help those people in dire need. You can shell out whatever little you can, maybe one percent of your salary. Even that would make a huge difference considering we are more than fifteen lakh people now. Do your research, find out the best NGO around your place and devote some time and money. True happiness lies in giving not receiving. Experience the inexperienced!"

Few days later, we added another point to our list, it was about education:

"Education is one of the most effective tool which can uplift the poor and lead to empowerment of the youth. All of us on this group are lucky to blessed with it. But there are millions of others in our country who are not. Education can go a long way in our country's development as the educated youth are the key for a prosperous India. I urge all of you to find some time off from your busy schedule to teach the under privileged section of the society. There are plenty of NGOs who need voluntary teachers like the 'Teach India' initiative from 'The Times of India' and there are many more. So here again do you research and find some time for these people. Your effort will not go waste."

Meanwhile, the sales of our magazine kept soaring and the money kept pouring. We were earning more money than our salaries put together. I guess leaving our jobs was the wisest decision we had taken. But it really wasn't about the money; that was just the icing on the cake.

One morning as I was reading the newspaper, I was thrilled to say the least. There was a small article about our magazine and our group in their supplement. The article read:

"Unique ways of improving the country:

Not so long ago, a bunch of guys had created a group on facebook called 'The India I dream of'. Barely a month later there are more than 15 lakh members on the page. The administrators of the group talk about doing their part to improve the country. There is a list of around ten points which every member of the group vows to follow. And now the same people have published a magazine 'The India I dream of'. This one too has the same purpose. What is intriguing to note here is that people from all over the country contribute to the articles that are published. These people then choose the articles deserving maximum public attention.

It is amazing that such selfless people are still a part of this society. They have spread the act of goodwill and now the whole country is getting involved. We wish them all the best."

Wow, I thought. Just then Nikita called.

"Hey did you read that article about us?" Nikita said, more elated and excited than me.

"Yeah baby, just read it. Isn't that wonderful?"

"Oh my god, I don't believe this, we are getting famous now."

"Yes we are."

I could hear a faint beep in the background. I looked at the phone. It was Dev.

"Hey just hang on a second Nikita, Dev is calling, I'll just put him on line."

I initiated a conference call and all three were on line.

"Hey guys," Dev was yelling, "you know what?"

"Yeah we know," I and Nikita beamed together, "the article right?"

"No! Not that! I just got a call from 104.5 FM radio! These guys are calling us for an interview. They want to know about us and transmit it on air. Imagine so many people would get to know about us."

"Wow man, that's wonderful."

"Great, this is lovely." I said.

It sure was. The manager of the radio channel spoke to us later that day and fixed a meeting with us few days later. Till then we could hear the innumerous times the radio jockeys spoke about the show to make all their listeners aware.

On the day of the interview, two hours before our time, we were there. We had to follow the punctuality part of our list. The office of the radio channel was a measly one. It was inside a huge building which was adorned with huge satellite dishes over its roof. As we entered the office, we walked through the long alleyway that had little rooms on its either side. We could see the respect in the eyes of the people for us. It felt great.

We met the radio jockey who would interview us an hour later. We introduced our selves to him. He was a tall, lean man and had a gift of gab; I guess the pre requisite of this job. He guided us about the interview and made us comfortable. And sharp eight, it began.

"Hello ladies and gentlemen, I am your RJ Ayush. Today with me I have those three people who created the idea of "The India I dream of" and more recently the magazine. They have made us all introspect and look within us before we complain and criticize the society, our politicians and our country. They want that every individual of this country to change first. And as all of you know guys, it is working, bloody well working. With more than 20 lakh fans on the facebook and 5 lakh copies of the magazine already sold, I like you to welcome Harsh, Dev and Nikita."

"Thanks Ayush, it's a pleasure to be here." I said, I guess I was the leader.

"So guys tell me, how does it feel to be known and read by so many people? We are talking about 2 million people here."

"It's wonderful, but you know we never had any idea this would go that far, all we had expected were a few people, maybe our friends, their friends and that's about it."

"And what triggered this idea?"

I looked at Nikita, maybe she would like to answer that. But Dev took over.

"Well let's just say we had a real bad nightmare one day that we were living in a country full of poverty, filth and unemployment. When we woke we thought we have to do something, but once we started, there wasn't any looking back," Dev looked at me and patted on my back. "Well to be honest with you, it was this guy's idea; I and Nikita condemned it in the beginning. Like everybody else we always thought it was futile, nobody would care about it. But we were so wrong, guess people in this country have now started caring, they want to see changes and most importantly they want to act, they want to be responsible and do their part."

"Well sure we all can see that," Ayush replied, "from the thousands of 'asshole' videos on youtube to the heavy traffic on your blogs and your group, people rushing to help each other out; it surely is working. Trust me even I stop at all red lights now, shunned my habit of throwing trash on roads and would love to help others in need. You guys have made a difference in the mindset of so many people and the number is rising all the time."

"Yeah true," it was Nikita this time, "the idea of the 'asshole' videos was really funny. Initially it was not really an idea, just an action that happened at the spur of the moment. But once we started, it really took off. It excited so many people and so many videos were being posted every day. I guess that has scared people, they watch out for their actions before doing anything immoral. And as far as the helping goes, really we never thought it could work. People in India don't have time for them, forget for others. Here again we were proved wrong, we get so many mails and posts everyday from people all over the country benefiting from this. People have really started taking interest and genuinely want to help. It is amazing."

"Yeah," I added, "and you know what had it not been for facebook and the internet, this idea would have just disappeared without a trace."

"Sure," the RJ replied, "we all owe it to that. And how about the magazine guys, where did that come from?"

"Yeah the magazine," I said with pride, "well to tell you the truth, it was not our idea, but a girl from Bhubaneshwar named Priya had suggested this idea. It was basically a way to reach millions of other people who were either not aware of us or the ones that were not really a net person, like I was a couple of months ago."

"Hmm…and what exactly is the idea behind this magazine?"

"Well, it is similar to its online counterpart," Dev said, "here people write articles which require attention; we just select the most important ones and publish them. Other than that we have a list of 10 people with the best and worst deeds. It is an attempt to make these people famous, appreciate the good ones and well kick the other ones. Apart from this we motivate people by including facts and figures about the development of the country. The idea is straight, don't get demoralized by the corruption and poverty, every country has its problems, we together have to sort it out and not depend on some invisible power to do it."

"That is so wonderful and inspiring at the same time guys, I'm sure all the people listening to you at the moment think likewise."

"Thanks." the three of us said in unison.

"Hey so before you guys bid adieu, any message you would want to leave?"

"Yeah sure," said Nikita, "I would just say that no country is perfect, it has to be made one. If you think it's only India which is in this mess, you are mistaken; all countries have their flaws, so be positive and do your part."

"For all of you who are not on the group, please be a part of 'The India I dream of' and follow the list religiously. Slowly but steadily we would surely make a change" said I.

"And last but not the least do grab a copy of our magazine. Keep sharing your ideas, keep recording the assholes, make them famous and let's all help each other in need. " Dev spoke the finishing lines.

We bade our goodbyes to the team and the manager. It felt great to be able to communicate with so many people. We felt special; we were not ordinary people anymore. We were being interviewed, our articles publish in news papers, we had millions of fans; I guess we were anything but ordinary people.

22

THE PROTESTS....

IT was a bright Sunday morning as I awoke slowly. Over the last few weeks my morning ritual had changed. I had to switch on my computer and log on to facebook to check out interesting and inspiring posts. My morning couldn't have been better today. I was delighted to see the following post:

"Hey guys, I am Anurag from Bhopal. Like all of you I am a fan of this page and of Harsh. What a brilliant platform this is to make a change in the country. I am here to talk about the latest article Harsh has covered in his yet another wonderful idea- his magazine. It is sad to observe the corruption in the Public Distribution System. People are embezzling the rights of the subsidized products from the poor so that they can make money out of it. I guess corruption has reached a crescendo in this country now and it needs to be addressed urgently. I have decided I am not going to keep quiet about it. What about you guys???

I have planned to be outside the district magistrate's office protesting for the above on the coming Monday at

11 A.M. Please guys I urge people of Bhopal and from neighbouring cities to join me in this ordeal. Harsh has showed us the way, now it's time for us to act. Let's not depend only on our police and government; we all know how they work. If we want a better India, we have to do something.

I'll see you guys on Monday for the protest.

Anurag

P.S. – Be the change you want to see in INDIA. "

Wow! That was gratifying. If enough people can be there, it can be a good story, I thought.

A day later, there were 6523 comments on the post already. What was even overwhelming was the fact that so many people had accorded with Anurag and promised to be there protesting for the rights of the poor!

✽ ✽ ✽ ✽

Two days later, there were links posted on our group page about the videos on the youtube regarding the protest. We clicked on it and were surprised. There were atleast a thousand people on the roads protesting and demanding justice outside the district magistrate's office. The comments below motivated more and more people nearby to join them.

The next day we were excited yet again. We were at Dev's place and were celebrating the success of our magazine. The story we had covered about the PDS in Madhya Pradesh was being telecast on a prominent news channel. A famous news reporter was covering it. The journalist who had sent us the information was also in the news and so were the thousands of my fans protesting and complaining about the system.

The story had become viral on the internet and television. Over the next few hours it was being covered on almost every news channel. The officials who were behind the scam were being interviewed and slowly but steadily the movement was gaining momentum. We weren't sure what the final outcome would be, but as long as the story had come out in the open and people wanted to make a change, it was a job well done.

However the result was an eye-opener for us. A few days later, an FIR had been lodged against the sub-divisional magistrate and the block development officer for theft and embezzlement of funds and a detailed investigation was in place to arrest all others behind the scam.

Life couldn't have been more wonderful and rewarding.

But it got better!

Justice was given in a similar way in the MNREGA corruption story in Jodhpur as was in our first story. A gentleman named Samrat from Jodhpur created an event on our group called 'A march against corruption'. He added the date and asked his fellow residents to protest outside the District Program Coordinator of MNREGA.

It was like déjà vu. An exact repeat of events is what took place. People took to streets, they were protesting and screaming. Just when the story garnered some limelight, the media took over, after which it became huge. The investigation and the trial were impending but already all of us were too optimistic.

We were too pumped up by the way justice was given to our stories; that made us post the following comment on our group page:

"Hey guys, so many of us have seen the way action was taken against the corrupt. Apart from the magazine, I guess the real contributors are you people who gave us such brilliant and deserving articles. Not to forget the initiative taken by so many people to be part of the protest and make justice happen. All that put a lot of pressure on the concerned authorities and there was no way justice could have been denied.

So for all the other articles in the magazine, may I request you all to come and protest together? I was thinking the people of the city in which the story is based have to take it as their moral duty to be a part of the protest. I can assure you if there are enough people doing that, media would take over which will make justice come soon. So please be there to fight together.

Delhites catch us for any protest in Delhi. We'll definitely be there.

Will you?"

Over the next few weeks, we were called for interviews by various newspapers, both regional and national. We were also on television and lauded for covering the stories and doing a heads up for so many stories deserving attention.

Our interviews were all over you tube. It felt as if we were celebrities, where ever we went people knew us. They took our photographs, got them clicked with us.

We made a decision – to make our magazine a monthly issue and that we would gradually increase the number of stories in the magazine. For the coming month, we had planned to have five of them and thereafter every month atleast ten. This way more and people could get justice. Maybe we were getting impatient.

The next few days we kept reading mails from thousands, rather millions of our fans suggesting stories. I don't know about others, but we were very clear about our first story.

It had to be about that cop Brajesh Singh.

23

THAT DREADFUL NIGHT!

"IT was around midnight when three friends – Sneha, Rahul and Bharat(names changed on request) were driving back home to Delhi from Meerut after attending their friend's wedding. Midway towards their destination, Rahul had an urge to smoke.

Few minutes later they stopped at a small dilapidated shop at the corner of a dreary road to grab a pack of cigarettes. Suddenly a drunk police officer (he had a bottle of rum in his hand and he was on duty) emerged from behind and began confronting and abusing them. He began questioning them what were they upto in the middle of the night, rather roughly. Sneha lost her patience and told him she would complain as he was drunk on duty. That incited the cop and he slapped her so hard that she fell on the road. Blood oozed from her nostrils and she found hard to breathe. On seeing this, Rahul demanded the officer reasoning for his action and said they had done nothing wrong. The cop in a fit of rage held his neck and called his two constables to put them in the jeep and took them to the nearest police station. He said something like he would misuse his power to teach these guys a lesson.

In the police station, the three of them were put behind the bars. This action was not justified according to the Indian Penal Code. But that was a very small misuse of power the cop had done. The worse was still to come.

Inside the locker, the three of them were agitated and wondered what they could do next. They decided to call their parents and take their advice, maybe call a lawyer or somebody to assist. As they took out their phone, the cop Brajesh came running towards them, opened their lock up and snatched the phone from them. He took the other two phones as well so they couldn't communicate. That again was a misuse of power. The three of them kept saying that it was their right to call but no one paid a heed. He came out with the phones and locked them again.

"Sir please you can't do this to us, atleast let us call." Bharat pleaded from inside.

"Fuck you behenchod," the cop replied.

"Sir this is wrong, you can't put us in lockup like that, we haven't done anything wrong." Rahul said.

"Don't you motherfuckers tell me what is right or wrong, you understand that?"

"Sir please, let us go, this is not fair." Bharat said.

"You guys question me, Brajesh, a police officer, you don't know what I can do with you, stay here for the entire night, only then will you learn a lesson," the cop said, inebriated. It was certainly a question of his ego now.

"Sir but how can you keep us here all night, what wrong have we done, this is injustice," Bharat said, his tone was a bit loud.

"Oye behenchod, I'm warning you don't tell me what I can do, now I am only keeping you here, one more word and I will bash you so hard, you will remember for the rest of your life." The cop grew furious.

"How can you bash us just like that," Rahul yelled in asperity, "you don't have the right to do that without any reason."

"You fuckers would not learn like that huh, wait," he turned around and walked in a rage towards a constable. He snatched the thick stick from his hands and came back in their cell.

"What were you saying behenchod?" he was yelling directly to Rahul now, "I can't bash you, take this motherfucker." He started hitting Rahul with his stick. Rahul fell on the floor and began screaming but the cop didn't stop.

"Now why don't you say something bastard?"

"Sir please stop, he'll get hurt." Bharat demanded from behind.

The cop in a fit of rage began slamming the stick towards Bharat now. He too fell on the floor. Brajesh hit them alternatively on their entire body. Both of them screamed in pain but that didn't stop him. Both of them had told Sneha not to utter a word so that he doesn't do any harm to her. She had controlled her all this while but looking at the blood on their shirts, she couldn't stop herself.

"What are you doing, they are bleeding now, please stop this madness," she shouted.

"Nobody tells me to stop, understand you bitch, get lost." He pushed her behind, grabbing her breasts. "They are soft, ha, ha". And then he continued moving his stick back and forth. The screams continued and so were the abuses.

Sneha couldn't believe what just happened. She was in a police station inside the cell and a police officer misbehaved with her. She had not experienced that even on the roads.

"What is wrong with you officer, how could you do that, how dare you touch me like that?" she demanded.

"What?" Brajesh stopped hitting them now. He turned towards her and spoke directly looking into her eyes that were lustful and fiery at the same time. "What did you just say you fucking bitch?"

"I said how can you touch me like that, I will report this and get you punished."

"What?" the cop was laughing now. "Hey Mahesh did you hear that?" he looked towards his constables and even they were laughing. "This bitch will get me punished, ha, ha, ha."

"Teach her a lesson sahib, she'll know," one of the ugly looking constable advised.

"You bitch; you don't know who are you messing with? Not only am I in charge here, but my brother is MLA of this area. I can kill you all here and bury you outside and nobody will ask any question, you understand that. This is not Delhi, you are in Uttar Pradesh, this is our state." And this time he moved his lustful hands on her arms and then on her breasts, squeezing them.

Sneha moved away in disgust, "you are one bastard," she said, "you don't know my father, I'll get you arrested."

The cop couldn't take that anymore. "That's it, I have to teach you a lesson now." He held her arms tight and yanked her outside forcefully towards his seat. Sneha tried to resist, but he was too strong for her.

"Hey stop, where are you taking me?" she continued yelling and tried to release her arms.

The cop didn't reply, just kept pulling her.

"Hey what is he doing now?" Bharat asked Rahul. Both had blood all over their faces and found it hard to speak.

"I don't know, I hope she'll be fine." Rahul moaned.

They tried getting up and stopping Brajesh, but they were emasculated of all their strength due to the blows. They could not see Sneha anymore, just heard her screams and the laughter of the constables.

"Please stop, don't do this to me," she was screaming hard but no one listened.

Rahul and Bharat could hear the ranting of Brajesh now and the high pitched cry of Sneha.

"Oh my god what is he doing to her?" Rahul sreamed. Bharat had tears in his eyes. He tried getting up and wanted to stop the injustice. But he could barely move.

The moaning of Brajesh had increased and so were the screams of Sneha. Ten minutes later, Sneha emerged in sight of Rahul and Bharat. She looked dull and lost. She couldn't stop weeping and walked towards them.

Brajesh came out and tucked his shirt in his pants and pulled up his zips. "So how was it bitch, ha, ha?"

Sneha didn't utter a word and opened the door of the cell and sat at the far corner of the room. She hid her head with her arms and wept continuously.

Brajesh came towards them. "Listen you mother fuckers now, that bitch has got the lesson of her life. One more word from you and I swear I'll kill you all. And remember one more thing, if you tell this to anyone after I release you, whatever happens to me but I'll make sure I will come to your homes one by one at the address mentioned in your driving licences and kill your parents infront of you first and then you. So shut up and don't dare raise your voice against me, ever."

174 og *The India I Dream of*

And then he was gone. In the morning the constable opened the lock up and set them free. Sneha couldn't sleep all night. Her eyes had become black and pudgy due to the tears. She didn't spoke to both of them. Two hours later they finally reached Delhi and didn't speak to anyone about this.

It's been more than five months after the incident, but still no one is aware of it. They decided to keep it to themselves otherwise it would have bought a lot of humiliation to Sneha.

Do the powerful people in this country really have that much power? Can they do anything and get away with it. We are talking about a police officer raping a woman in his own police station as the other constables watched in enjoyment. The three of them did not report anything as they knew he had enough power and would get away with it. What have we become? I urge all of you to not be quiet and report these kinds of instances regularly so that action can be taken against all those who think the laws of the country are not meant for them."

Tears ran through our eyes as we finalized the words of the incident that changed our world that day. Nikita left for her home as she couldn't take it anymore. That's it, we had thought, we won't spare that asshole anymore. With the villains of our stories in the first issue of our magazine behind the bars now we were sure justice won't be denied to us any longer.

We finalized the other four stories for our issue along with the list of the 'assholes' and the 'good deeds'. Next week the magazine would be out and with that the deeds of that cop.

We so wanted justice.

24

THE BEGINNING.....

ONE of the biggest woes of Uttar Pradesh is notoriety and depredation of its police force. The U.P. police have always been in bad shape. False encounter deaths, under-reporting of crime for a better crime statistics, arbitrary transfer of police officers, rapes in police custody are pervasive in this part of the country.

Perhaps that was the reason for the angst and despair of the people of this state which resulted in mass protests across the entire state. Our story in the magazine about a girl being raped inside a police station by the police officer in charge as sub-inspectors and constables watched, took the nation by surprise.

This was not something unusual; instances like this are ubiquitous in this state. However never before had such an incident got such widespread publicity. Flat five days after the second issue of the magazine was published, our story was already being covered over all news channels. Whatever publicity of the event we lacked was taken care by the news channels by blowing it out of proportion.

This initially started by my post on our group page:

"Hello everybody, the article about the rape of a girl in police custody in Uttar Pradesh is alarming. I am sure all of you who have read the second issue of our magazine would think likewise. Let's all stand united to curb this menace that gnaws our society. Let's show the powerful in our country what the common men can do. We have thought about a demonstration against these corrupt public servants in Uttar Pradesh; let us stage a march to protest against these shocking issues in this state.

Tell us what you think of the same. A 'like' would indicate your approval. If we receive more than ten thousand 'likes', we will confirm the date of the march.

Eagerly awaiting your response!

Regards,

Harsh

P.S. – Be the change you want to see in INDIA."

The result was both astonishing and satiating. Less than twenty four hours later, the date of the march was already decided. It took just about sixteen hours for the ten thousand likes. We created an event on our group – "A march for justice" along with the date.

On 26th of December, thousands of people marched in various cities of Uttar Pradesh – Kanpur, Allahabad, Ghaziabad, Lucknow, Meerut, Agra, Moradabad, Varanasi and others. Within hours of the march, media began covering it on television and thousands of others unaware of this became a part of this unrest.

Women empowerment NGOs across the state joined us in this protest. It was no more a personal anguish anymore but tens of thousands of people had joined us. This is exactly what I had wanted a few months back when doing my part for the country had first occurred to me. The incident on the day of Ankit's marriage had only fostered my thought. I was so unclear then, I knew exactly what I wanted to do, but never knew how and when.

This is still like a dream to me. I could have never imagined the turn of events this way, that too when only about a few months ago I was recovering from those ghastly images and voices in my head. I am still not over them though, but still I am proud of myself and over all the guilt that was lurking somewhere within me that I couldn't help Nikita that day.

I'm sure even Nikita would be in a much better state of mind now considering what she had to go through. I still remember how I thought I had lost her forever. She was leaving for America to do her MBA leaving behind all the forlorn memories of that night inside the police station. I was sure I would never see her again once she left the country. My love for her had no meaning then, it was way too small compared to her miseries. But she is a strong person, the very fact she joined me in my endeavour justifies that. I was so glad she didn't leave India and more importantly, me!

Dev – he is such an asshole and will always be. But he did the most important thing in my life - created my facebook account. Had it not been for that, I'm sure this would only have been a dream. What began as a fervent midnight post on facebook in my frustrated mind led to one of the craziest, unprecedented protests our country had ever seen. I'm so glad Dev did that and so grateful to Mark Zuckerberg for creating Facebook!

✳ ✳ ✳ ✳

T he march had become so famous that the entire country was aware of it as it was covered on all news channels – English, Hindi, regional as well the radio channels. There was a lot of pressure on the police department of Uttar Pradesh. An action by them was inevitable so as to save their image.

In 2010 when Mayawati was the Chief Minister of the state, she had issued an order so as to improve the system, that rape shall be considered as a special report case and all rape cases had to be investigated by a high ranking police officer of DIG (Deputy Inspector General of Police) or IG (Inspector General of Police) rank. Earlier this was considered only as an ordinary crime which was monitored only by the circle officer.

Just two days after the march, taking a serious note of the incident, the Inspector General of the range had ordered a probe into the case and asked the DIG of the zone to take over the case. An FIR had been lodged against the police inspector Brajesh Singh and his subordinates under various sections of the IPC code.

In addition to Brajesh Singh, an FIR was issued against his MLA brother too for cases of corruption, black marketing, rapes and even murders.

We breathed a sigh of relief. We finally tasted success.

Or did we?

Well, this was just the beginning!

EPILOGUE

I had never believed in the power of facebook. Hell I never even had an account until few months ago when Dev and Nikita – my best friends from school - coaxed me into having one. I had always thought it was meant for introverts who lived in an apparent world restricted within their own shell.

I mean how else could someone explain facebook chatting with people whom you never even meet or talk in the *real* world unless you were Dev who would use it as a tool to attract girls for a date? Psycho really!!!

I completely hated the idea of spending hours scrolling through the pictures of friends or maybe friends' friends who are complete strangers to me vacationing and ostentatiously displaying it on their profile. What was the idea behind it?

Had to be show off, I presumed. How would other people know how much fun one is having or maybe it was an attempt to make their friends jealous of their merrymaking trips? I didn't see any other explicable reason behind it.

Weird right!

Wrong.

Well at least for the last few months.

❊ ❊ ❊ ❊

A year had passed after that incident. Life had completely changed for the three of us and well also for a lot of Indians. It had been little more than six months now since the first issue of our magazine was published. Six more issues had been published after that. Over 50 new cases came out in the open which were hidden all this while. More than half of them already got the desired results and more than hundred people are in prison because of the same including Brajesh Singh.

There are 54,45,890 members on the group now. I could never believe that number. The total Indians on facebook are in excess of 3 crores, so well still there is a lot of scope for improvement. Any comment by anyone on the group page receives atleast ten thousand comments on an average. There are around twenty thousand 'asshole' videos on youtube now. More than half of the members on the group are contributing part of their salary to NGOs or finding time to teach under privileged children. India was changing now, I could see that.

We three were nominated for the 'youth icon' of the country. The event would be next week. We definitely would be going there. But the result won't matter to us. I know we were the youth icons anyway; we had changed so many people.

I was blogging more than ever. They too received over five grand comments on each. We had also become quite wealthy, our magazine and my blogs gave us a lot of money. However we were contributing half of that money to NGOs now. We don't need that much anyway. Mahatma Gandhi had once said - "there is enough in the universe for everyone's need, but not greed." We had got much more than we ever wanted.

I felt like writing; that was the best way of expressing my feelings. I took out my laptop and started typing on my blog at blogger.com:

"Not very long ago, I hated India and everything about it - the corruption and scandals, population and pollution, illiteracy and unemployment, et al. It never occurred to me, that I, as a citizen of this country had not been a good citizen myself, then how on earth was I expecting the country to be good to me. I had been an asshole like the many others I had made famous. I had never voted, I used to drink and drive causing accidents, peed on roads and for all those thousands of videos uploaded daily on youtube, I can say I was one of them. Then what could I possibly be complaining about?

Life can be a bitch if you treat her like one.

It was!

I used to always think that no good can be achieved by the action of a single person. The last year has been a testament to my erroneous thought. It really has proved to be a cracker of a year. I still remember it was just an idea in the agitated and restless mind of mine when I had turned to facebook. And since then, there's no looking back. We are more than 5 million people now and that's what makes this journey special.

We still have a long way to go though, nevertheless, the journey has been great so far.

I urge all of you to believe in yourself and your actions; stand up for your right and make this country a perfect one.

Remember it's never too late for anything in life.
Harsh
19 July 2012
P.S. – Be the change you want to see in India."

Truly the last year had been a cracker of a year. There is hardly any feeling left that we haven't experienced. But it feels good now, infact much better than that. Life is best when you can see results of your actions.

Our thing had changed Dev as well. He was no more the 'asshole' we had termed him. However his last girlfriend also got married.

To him!

There was another thing that was troubling me for a lot of days. I had still not conveyed my feelings to Nikita. Now that we were together all the time, she should agree. However that incident had changed her. I never knew what I could expect from her.

I picked up the phone. My heart raced.

I dialed her number!

ACKNOWLEDGEMENT

A<small>FTER</small> reading about 200 pages of the book, I hope you have the patience to read another page of my unassuming thank you note.

Firstly, I would sincerely hope you liked the book and my earnest attempt to instill some pride and belief in our country that is full of scams and corruption. Well to be honest, it's not too bad. Do join the group "The India I dream of" on facebook and *be the change you want to see in India*.

It's been a wonderful time ever since my first novel "When life tricked me" was published. Honestly, the love and appreciation I garnered from it enthused me in writing this one. Keep that coming my wonderful readers!!

And now for some moral obligations:

I like to thank my friends and family for their unconditional love and support throughout. My team at Srishti who publish books in record time and most importantly my readers and my little family on facebook! In particular, I would like to thank the following for their regular messages and comments and motivating me to continue writing:

184 ca Acknowledgement

Harshvardhan Nahata, Jas Dhanota, Ritu Sethi, Nikita Bali, Shrishti Shrivastava, Pallavi Bains, Jaya Chetwani, Manish Dalwani, Remo Rajesh, Charmi Madia, Vishal Saxena, Sonia Sason, Chetan Joshi, Niyanta Patel, Laxmi Panigrahi, Shashank Maheshwari, Savio Paes, Tajinder Arora, Shals Castelino, Ankit Wani, Sonam Shringar, Arpan Singh, Simran Peters, Kevin Abrey, Rehan Quereshi, Shingu Jais, Deepak Chandel, Aarti Yadav, Anushka Lal, Megha Das, Mamta Verma, Mohnish Singh, Ritu Sethi, Meghana Meghu, Kajal Agarwal, Karan Bali, Aditya Shrivastava, Nancy Arora, Shalene Thallapaka, Gurparkash Singh, Mandeep Mistry, Sanamdeep Singh, Tanvi Nuwal, Vydya, Anuj Garg, Chetna Deharia, Sam Rocky, Gnanendra Reddy, Laxmi Mallampati, Ankur Chaturvedi, Esha Majumder, Kanika Khanduja, Deep Roy, Dipika Makhija, Samrat Malhotra, Puja Jain, Priyanka Patel, Dilip Mahajan, Kirti Tyagi, Rishabh Parakh, Nagendra Singh, Mrinmoy Kashyap, Ruchi Raghuwanshi, Paddus, Ubhay Singh, Gaurav Gupta, Pritesh Upadhyay, Prerna Kandoi, Onkar Grover, Gautam Shitole, Nimisha Arya, Rosa Priya, Niraj Kumar, Sonam Bajaj, Anurag Bhandari, Irfaan Kamraaz, Manisha Rao, Ashok Andhale, Randeep Reddy, Pratiksha Karpe, Dheera Jaiswal, Ruth Roy, Khushboo Jain, Arpita Mukherjee, Pooja Chopda, Aparajita Mukherjee, Karthik Gururaj, Sapna Sharma, Gaurav Das, Anandika Kaushal, Rashika Singh, Nida Pathan, Anupma Singh.

And lastly as I said last time, I like to thank my profession, for providing me with abundance of peace and tranquility in all the huge and wonderful oceans of the world. One can seldom find that living in the metros of India!!!